Connecting the Doubts

by Alex Mayberry

For Emma, Gemma, Karen, Katie, and Susan.
I love you all.

1

'Fuck you, bitch.'

That was the last thing Tanya had said before Bobbi made for her and the rest of the girls had to physically intervene. Had Lucy and Claire not been blocking her, the night would have been far, far worse. As it was, it was bad enough, making this morning's aftermath all the shittier.

She was still wearing her top from the previous night, the smell of stale smoke filling her nostrils as her senses started to twitch into life. Usually after a night out, she would have rewarded herself for ignoring the siren calls of the kebab shop with a slice of Nutella on toast. Not this time though. The night had turned out to be such an ordeal that all she had wanted to do, having reached home, was sink into the cool arms of her unmade bed.

Lying there now Bobbi realised that the drink from the night before wasn't causing the pounding in her head, although that certainly wasn't helping matters. Rather, it was the conclusion of last night's events, mercilessly replaying in her mind, like someone thumping the window of a car that had plunged into water. With each desperate thud, the next more intense than the last, blood swarmed into Bobbi's cheeks until eventually, the glass ceded. As the flood of memory came pouring through, the intensity of feelings, temporarily sedated by sleep, were suddenly revived.

'Fuck, you...'

She said the words out loud and slowly, her lips slightly sticking together. Silently, she completed the recital, mouthing the word 'bitch.' They were mean words, ugly in the intent behind them. Annoyed didn't really come close to covering how Bobbi felt right now, but there was more to it than that. There was embarrassment, undoubtedly, about the way her friend had acted, but in time, there would also be fear. Had she deserved it? What if, harboured within the phrase, there was a slight prickle of truth?

'What the hell was she thinking?' thought Bobbi.

At some point, her own part in the night's drama would have its chance to take the stage. For now, despite anger beginning to well within her again, the effects of last night's alcohol and the natural drowsiness of waking up were restraining the outpouring of full-blown annoyance. The first murmurs of the tsunami though had begun to menacingly lap at the shoreline between her thoughts and her tongue.

'Friend,' her mind spat. The sharpness of the word nicked away at her mental bonds until they snapped.

'Fuck me!' she blurted out incredulously, slamming her hand on the mattress in frustration at just how unbelievable the night had turned out.

She lifted her head, but a swift jolt of pain embedded in her temple soon put paid to any thoughts of movement. Almost instinctively, she flipped the pillow, plunging her face into the coolness it offered.

This hangover had every chance of being her worst one since that work do a few years back. It was rarely spoken of these days, either out of embarrassment or respect depending on who you asked. Like then, last night at the time had seemed like a good idea, but then again it always does. Bobbi often enjoyed a drink but there's a difference between having a glass or two at home in front of the telly and being out, when the only answer to the offer of a shot is 'pass the salt and lime.' She wasn't getting any younger too if that wasn't obvious enough already. Regardless, Bobbi had certainly made the most of the opportunity the evening presented. Claire had a lot to do with that, though Bobbi hadn't needed much encouragement.

Bobbi typically dealt with things in a matter-of-fact kind of way, protecting herself against the rocks of disappointment that life would sometimes hurl her way with a shield of sarcasm. She had her dad's humour, although unlike him, she wasn't a joke teller. He needed no invitation to tell a gag, gleefully unloading one of his classics whenever he met someone new or was retelling one to either Bobbi or her mum when the mood took him.

The first time her dad met Mike, he put him on the spot straight away by asking him to tell a joke. Bobbi had neglected to prepare him, despite her dad pulling the same trick with every boyfriend who came to their house since she was fifteen. Fortunately,

Mike had one up his sleeve.

'Why should you only borrow money from pessimists?'

Bobbi's dad shook his head.

'Because they'll never expect you to pay it back.'

A slap on the shoulder and a nod towards Bobbi suggested Mike had passed his test.

'Would you like a beer, Michael?' he said over his shoulder, on his way to the kitchen.

Unfortunately, this situation with Tanya was something altogether different, and not the sort of thing that could be easily excused with a shrug of the shoulders or a moment of mirth. The shock had been beyond intense, releasing a spike of adrenaline that only dissipated once the taxi had deposited Bobbi outside her front door. Her energy depleted, on autopilot she'd downed a glass of water, poured another for the morning, and managed a quick wee before crawling between the crumpled sheets of her bed.

2

'I got the one that was on offer at Woolworths,' he said.

As far back as she could remember, Bobbi had had a slightly pessimistic outlook on life. When she was eight, she overhead her dad talking to her mum in the kitchen while on her way to grab a bag of crisps.

'Is it a Barbie?' mum whispered back.

Bobbi's eyes and ears leapt in shock at the sound of that name. She quickly darted back into the doorway of the adjacent room. She stood silently, far enough away to be undetected, but close enough to hear the not-so-secret conversation as it turned out. Dad was making no apparent effort to prevent his voice from falling into the ears of would-be eavesdroppers.

'No. It's err, it's better than that.'

'Phil!' said Jan.

'What?' he said defensively. 'They're all the same, aren't they?'

'You know she's been talking about that one for ages. Does it have a wand and crown?'

'No,' he said, 'but it's got a dog,' he shot back. 'Leads look a bit like wands,' he said unconvincingly.

Jan shot her husband a disapproving look.

'Look,' he said indignantly, his voice rising slightly, 'have you seen those prices, Jan?'

She shooshed him by grabbing his arm.

'Keep it down, she'll hear you.'

Glancing round, and sensing a softer tact was needed, he rubbed Jan's arm reassuringly, pulling her closer to him.

'She'll like it,' he said, his tone quieter and plain. 'Don't worry. It'll be fine.'

Jan looped her arms around his neck and looked at him directly. Her eyes softened.

'It better be love. She doesn't get much you know.'

'It'll be fine, honest,' said Phil. 'Are you making a brew, hun?'

She tutted but kissed him before turning away. Phil took the opportunity to playfully spank her backside, propelling a laugh to leap from Jan's mouth like ketchup being slapped from a bottle. She tried to hide it, but her lips stretched into a smile.

'Make yourself useful and get the biscuits out then,' she haughtily bossed.

Between the clinking of cups and the boiling of water, Bobbi heard her dad say that he'd stashed the gift behind the couch. A short time later, that is exactly where Bobbi found it, the familiar red lettering on the oversized white plastic bag not hard to miss.

Inside the bag, apart from the doll, Bobbi found an opened packet of chewing gum, a sheet of paper with printed numbers on, and a selection box. The cover of the box featured a grinning penguin wearing earmuffs and mittens, its arm cocked and loaded, ready to hurl a snowball at an unsuspecting seal. Had the gum been bubbalicious, Bobbi would have been tempted to take one, but it was spearmint, so she passed.

The blank expression on the doll's face mirrored the excitement on Bobbi's as she held the plastic box keeping the doll prisoner inside. Through the plastic, she could see a big yellow hat, along with the leader and dog that her dad had mentioned. Sindy's hair was platted, and the hat looked like a straw one mum had worn to a BBQ at her uncle's the previous summer. She remembered it rained that day, and the sight of her uncle attending the grill, standing under an umbrella. It was 'a typical British summer' as her dad liked to say.

Leaving the gift where she'd found it, Bobbi spent the rest of the day in her room. It dawned on her that this meant Santa wasn't real either. Her friend Stacey had already told her this at school, which Bobbi dismissed, calling her a big fat liar. Realising then though that it was true, she played glumly, wondering what else her mum and dad had lied to her about. The more she thought about things, the more upset she got until the sadness was too much and tears started to fall. Without knowing why, she decided not to discuss it with her parents, even when her mum had heard her sobs and came up to see what was wrong.

'Bad tummy?' her mum asked.

Bobbi nodded and that was that. Her parents likely assumed she'd discovered the truth from her friends, like Stacey who might have been right about Santa but was not related in any way to Kylie Minogue, proving she was a big fat liar about some things.

On Christmas morning, Bobbi opened her gifts, her heart resembling a balloon found three weeks after a party. She was surprised to also find an oversized pink comb and a doll sized vanity mirror in the box. With a big smile, she hugged her dad because she was grateful for the doll, and her other gifts. His presents were rubbish in comparison, but he didn't seem to mind. Mum was right that Bobbi didn't get a lot, but she noticed that her mum didn't either and so after that Christmas, Bobbi didn't ask for much. Her mum apologised that it wasn't the doll she'd wanted and so Bobbi gave her an extra-long hug to reassure her that she did in fact love it. Dad made a joke about the size of the brush and seeing him drag it over his closely cropped scalp made both Bobbi and Jan laugh.

'Silly sod,' said Jan, slapping Phil on the back.

'Silly sod,' repeated Bobbi.

Her dad turned towards her, the lines on his brow deepening.

'You what?' he said sternly.

Bobbi could only stare back, her mouth open, not knowing what to say or do. A grin then spread across his face as he lunged towards Bobbi and began tickling her ribs. Bobbi squealed uncontrollably, her legs and arms flailing around as if in spasm. Eventually it all became too much, and Bobbi accidently farted, sending her dad scurrying away to the safety of the kitchen.

A few weeks later, after seeing her mum give Phil a trim with the clippers, Bobbi stuck the mirror in Chloe's rigid hand, (she named the dog Sindy), and proceeded to deliver a less than even haircut to the defenceless doll. Poor Chloe wasn't played with much after that.

3

'Eh?' she grunted; her voice muffled.

Feeling an itch on her calf, Bobbi raised her opposite foot to address the irritant. The touch felt rough, and confusing. With one arm tucked under the pillow her face was smothering, her other arm cradled another pillow beside her. Opening her eyes was not a tempting prospect, but rather than delay the inevitable, she sharply forced them open and tilted her head. A tiny crack of light had breached the boundaries of the drawn curtains and caught Bobbi's face.

'Fuck off!!!' she complained, recoiling like a vampire from the sun, scurrying for cover beneath the sheets of her Egyptian linen coffin.

Within the dim light, Bobbi's eyes, encrusted with sleep, strained to focus. From the haziness of the space, a memory of sleeping over at a friend's house emerged. Thinking she was in her own bed she'd wake up completely disoriented from lying at the wrong end and staring up at an unfamiliar light shade.

The flashback dissipated when a feeling of airiness alerted her senses that she was in a state of undress, confirmed by using her left hand as a scanner. It found that the top couple of buttons on her blouse were undone. Bobbi's eyes were then shocked into focus as she glanced down to confirm that no skirt or pants had been felt. She'd always felt uncomfortable looking at her stomach, particularly after the caesarean, and tried to avoid doing so as much as possible. At home, baggy jumpers were deployed as a cloaking device, though one about as subtle as pink post-it notes.

Seeing the naked flesh of her thighs brought another shuddering jolt of reality to her temple. Bobbi sat up instantly, the sheet falling away to reveal the ghostly apparition hiding underneath. One shoe had managed to evade notice during her partial undressing, which now fell to the floor with a thud. That at least explained the roughness on her calf, she thought.

The dull shades of the room seeped into her retinas like sand flowing through a timer. The absent skirt and underwear were quickly located on the floor. They were Bobbi's special stretchy pants, a last-minute decision, inspired by the unconscious replaying of Bridget Jones in her head, to provide a little extra esteem boost.

'Not hard to miss,' she muttered, slapping herself with a jibe.

Mike always called them her 'big girl pants.'

'Listen, funny man,' she would say, 'I may wear big girl pants, but you wear little willy shorts.'

Mike always took her joke better than she took his. She knew it was only gentle teasing, and that he adored her body, much to her own incomprehension, yet she still couldn't help but let it hit home a little harder than it should have.

There were very few, if any, secrets between them, nothing important anyway, but this was something she would never openly admit to him. Knowing him, he would reign himself in, but in doing so, curtail their banter, which was the grease that kept their ship sailing as smoothly as it did. It's true that rain that falls in jest will still get you wet after all, but Bobbi preferred that to the perpetual desert of boring safe sunshine.

A small, framed photo, showing the two of them with their daughter, Louise, adorned the bedside cabinet. Lou Lou looked cute in the image despite the outfit she was wearing. Bobbi must have entrusted Mike's extensive knowledge of two-year-olds fashion that day, as her baby girl was sporting a random combination of jumper, shorts, tights, and wellies.

Mike was wearing a jumper his mum got him for his birthday, which didn't suit him at all. Neither the colour nor the fact that it emphasised his growing belly, flattered him. He was smiling though, his best smile no less.

Bobbi had always thought it was his best feature, drawing the attention of her eyes away from his attempts at what he deemed as stylish, back in those early dating days when they were both young and daft. The picture was a favourite of hers because in it, he was giving a dorky thumbs up. Bobbi had placed it by the bed, deliberately, so she could mock him with a similar salute before they turned off the lights. The gesture summed him up perfectly and she loved it.

She managed a smile as she looked at it. If he

could see her in this state, his arched eyebrows and smirking mouth would say everything without him having to speak.

'I know!' she said to the image, managing a chuckle before groaning as the pain in her temple struck again.

'Fuck' she moaned.

It was at that moment, truly hating her life, that Bobbi realised the smokiness of her top was being outstripped by the stench coming from her own mouth.

4

'Shit!' huffed Bobbi.

The digits on the bedside alarm were flashing, '00:00', in a neon green light. Bobbi vaguely recalled disconnecting the clock to plug the iron in. She slowly sat up and reached for the glass of water on the same bedside table. She gulped it down, grateful for her forward thinking. As she lay her head back, she closed her eyes and felt a tiny burp gurgle in her throat. She tried not to think about the gunk in her mouth she'd just swallowed.

'Thank goodness for stomach acid,' she thought.

Realising she had no clue what time it was, Bobbi grabbed her phone, relived to find it under her pillow where she usually kept it at night.

10:33 the phone told her silently.

In normal circumstances, she would have been up hours ago with Lou Lou. As it was half term, Mike had taken the week off to visit his mum in Scotland. They were going to stay in Ruth's caravan, which Lou Lou loved, not least because due to the lack of a TV, she would have the undivided attention of both her grandma and dad.

Bobbi couldn't take time off at the same time but if she was honest, she didn't mind missing out. Though she never said it directly, Bobbi always felt a slight but palpable sense that Ruth didn't approve when she and Mike got engaged. Five years of marriage later only served to convince Ruth, to

Bobbi's mind anyway, that her son had 'settled.' Mike would tease her paranoia, and it became a running joke between them. Fair to say then that the idea of being scrutinised, in a confined space for large parts of the day, didn't appeal all that much to her. Consequently, it meant that Bobbi would be in the unusual position of having the house to herself.

As they prepared to leave on Sunday evening, she'd felt a little anxious about how much she would miss them, but that lasted all of five minutes. Following hugs, and excited wave offs, Bobbi stretched out on the couch, soaking in the stillness and peace that filled the living room. She clicked on the remote, the TV buzzing into life with an array of colourful but noisy characters.

'Not today Mr Wolf,' she chuckled.

VH1 sprung out to her from the list of music channels, and so she clicked the button, joining a song in mid-chorus.

'It must have been love' she sang, using the remote as a mic, 'but it's over nowww.'

Two glasses of wine later, Bobbi had had a bath, ordered a Chow Mein, and was looking for a film to watch. It was a pity she had work the next day, as getting used to this freedom would be easy, she thought.

There were three missed calls: two from Alexis, and a text message, and one from Lucy.

'Nothing from Tanya then,' she thought.

She scrunched her nose up in defiance but couldn't help but feel a small wave of sadness wash over her. Alexis had sent the text at 7:15, as soon as she'd woken up Bobbi assumed. The message read:

'Hope you're ok. Let me know if you want me to come round for a chat. A.x'

'Not really,' thought Bobbi.

However, Mike and Louise weren't due back until tomorrow evening, so she had the day to relax before sorting the house out on Sunday. She texted back:

'Feel rough. Yes, please give me an hour thanks.x'

Bobbi closed her eyes and began to drift.

She hummed, 'Lay a whisper, on my pillow.'

Rubbing her eyes gently, Bobbi stretched.

'Some chocolate would be lovely now' she thought.

She was glad Alexis had messaged her, as she was the perfect person to talk to about the whole thing. Bobbi knew Alexis would tell her what had happened, without criticism or judgement. She glanced at her phone again, which showed that fifteen minutes had passed.

'Fuck!' she shouted, realising she'd better get a move on.

Bobbi slowly made her way to the bathroom and pulled the cord, sparking the bulb into life. After reaching for knickers that weren't there, she plonked herself down on the loo. Her head still ached, so she propped it up with her palm, her elbow grinding into her thigh.

She managed to concentrate enough to look at her phone again, scanning for anything from Tanya, but finding nothing. Her anger was less prominent now, as hunger started to rear its head, but it was still visible for those willing to look close enough, like bubbles in soup when it starts to boil.

The lack of a message, or more accurately an apology, from Tanya grated. A scroll through recent messages showed, to Bobbi's surprise, that the last message she had received from Tanya was over three weeks ago. Granted, they usually saw each other at work, but the last week had been particularly busy and so they hadn't. They typically called each other at least once a week too, but again, despite being on her own all week, Bobbi could only remember talking to her mum who was having a bother recording her soaps.

Bobbi tried to remember the last time she spoke to Tanya on the phone and came up blank. The text message itself was no use on its own. It simply read *'Ok,'* an acknowledgement of a context Bobbi was in no state of mind to recall right now.

Her phone buzzed again with a reply from Alexis.

'Be there at 12. Will bring cookies.x'

5

'Tanya!' shouted Alexis.

She couldn't believe the words she had just heard come out of the mouth of her friend. The outburst had similarly stunned the rest of the group. As Alexis turned, she held her breathe as she watched Bobbi. It took a few moments for her to absorb the impact, her face morphing from confusion, to hurt, back to confusion again, and then rage. A guttural, incoherent yell contorted her mouth, and as if possessed by a demonic force, she propelled herself towards Tanya, who now stood stunned into rigidity.

Lucy and Claire grabbed Bobbi's flailing limbs, as Alexis shepherded Tanya away to a position of safety. Tanya offered no resistance, following Alexis' commands to go with her as they hurriedly walked away. Without letting up her pace, Alexis glanced over her shoulder and could see that Bobbi was visibly and verbally agitated. The other women had released her but remained in her path, blocking while they attempted to sooth the beast that had been unleashed. Like a pair of fugitives fleeing a crime scene, Alexis and Tanya turned a corner, the sound of Bobbi's annoyance soon evaporating among the hum of traffic and the city.

They continued to move, turning another corner before crossing a road. Tanya had moved beyond the initial shock and was now slightly trembling. She began to weep.

'Come on,' said Alexis calmly, 'it'll all be

alright.'

Tanya could only offer a sniff and another sob in reply.

Alexis had phoned the taxi firm to rearrange their pick-up slot, which they now arrived at. It was a quieter area, away from the main rank in the busiest part of town. A young couple were occupying a nearby bench. The young woman had straddled the man's lap, and while they kissed, his hands explored her backside, ruffling her skirt and exposing her thong.

'Stop looking at her arse!' a woman yelled at the man with her, presumably her partner.

With a slap on his arm, he was immediately brought to heel, staring at the ground, and muttering his denials of wrongdoing. If the couple had heard her, they paid no attention and continued in their attempt to seemingly devour one another's tongues. Alexis, feeling a little uncomfortable with this brazen PDA, gestured to Tanya that they wait by the roadside.

The two women stood in silence now with Tanya having regained a degree of composure. The wetness of her tears had caused the little makeup she wore to smear. She looked up at Alexis' face now, like a dog left out on the back porch hoping to be let back indoors.

Tanya had an unfortunate tendency to assume people regarded her negatively and would usually be confident in this assessment. In that moment though, her face reading skills were off. She couldn't tell if

Alexis was angry or just trying extra hard to be her usual calm, composed self. Tanya decided to remain quiet, despite wanting to say something, though not sure what. Her head was all over the place, feeling both hurt and angry after the trigger that had tipped her over the edge.

She felt guilty too. She hated conflict. Subconsciously, the wheels of self-reassurance were working overtime. Alexis couldn't help but feel a little resentment building inside towards Tanya, which she didn't like. She wasn't the kind to deliberately ignore someone but satisfied herself that focussing on the road and looking out for their ride home was the best course of action right now.

The taxi duly arrived, and the two women climbed into the back. Alexis confirmed the address to the driver, and they were on their way. The taxi navigated the road that ran adjacent to the route they had all walked together a short time before. They passed the restaurant at the top end of the high street and then headed down to 'The Champagne Bar' just off the centre, the last place they'd been and close to where the group had split. Fifteen minutes had passed since they'd left the others and so Alexis wasn't surprised to see that the women had gone. She breathed a small sigh of relief.

Alexis glanced to her side to check on Tanya, but seeing her eyes were closed, quickly turned to face out of the window on her side. Tanya had her head back and was reciting a mantra internally to help control her breathing. She was managing to hold back the tears now that threatened to well in her eyes. The river would be let loose once she got home, but for now the dam was holding.

'Would you like to hear some music?'

The taxi driver up to this point had chosen to sit quietly, having deduced from his years of experience that this wasn't a happy party. The offer of music, he hoped, might lend a little levity, and help the atmosphere. Alexis pounced on the opportunity that a distraction from the silence offered.

'Yes please,' she replied, her face lighting up in tired glee.

The driver turned on the radio, which was tuned to a station dedicated to older music. The presenter ran through his spiel and played the next song, which began with a long warbled 'Wooh!' The warm raspiness of the singer's voice gave Alexis a chance to forget about Tanya for a moment. Her lips began to mime automatically but stumbled as the lyrics weren't quite what she expected. She leant forward to talk to the driver.

'Excuse me?'

He looked at her through his mirror.

'Sorry love,' he said, gesturing to her belt, 'would you mind putting that on please? It's just regulations and that.'

'Oh, of course,' replied Alexis, shuffling back to slot the buckle into place.

She tapped Tanya on the arm, who opened her eyes slowly. Tanya felt, and looked, in danger of drifting off now her nervous energy was beginning to dissipate. Alexis gestured to Tanya to do as she had but was dismissed by a waved arm and closed eyes. Alexis brushed off the rebuke and returned her attention to the driver, and her question.

'That's Michael Bolton isn't it?' she asked.

'What? Playing now?' the driver clarified.

'Yes, I'm pretty sure, it is,' she said.

'Noooo. It's Michael McDonald. Well,' he clarified, 'at the start it was James Ingram.'

'Ah, ok. I don't know who that is.'

He turned and looked at her quizzically.

'Have you not heard "Yah Mo B There" before?' The chorus kicked in and the driver sang along.

'Maybe,' she said. She listened closer.

'What's he saying? I will be there?'

'No, it's Yah Mo B There.'

Alexis laughed. 'Yamobie?'

Chuckling, the driver said, 'No, listen. Yah. Mo. Then B, the letter B.'

'Yah Mo B,' she repeated. 'What does that mean?'

'I think Yah is a shortened word, I forget what, but it means God. It's Hebrew, Jewish you know.'

'Well, I'd never have guessed that. How do you know that?'

The driver chuckled again.

'Well love, you don't get to my age without learning a few things along the way. Mostly useless information like, but it comes in useful now and again.'

'You should maybe join a quiz team,' she

suggested, 'or set one up yourself?'

'Ah well, yes I've done that in the past,' he said, 'but I, err, don't anymore.'

Something in his tone suggested this was a sore point. The music filled the void in conversation as Alexis briefly considered whether to pursue the topic. Before she could decide, the driver spoke again.

'So, you're a Michael Bolton fan?' he asked, his voice cheery and light again.

'Not sure I'd call myself a fan. I didn't join a club or anything or have posters of him on my wall. I like his voice though and know some of his songs.'

'I see,' he said. 'Who did you have on your wall?'

'Ah, well…I've always loved the icons of the Eighties.'

'Ok, I see,' he nodded.

'Yeah,' she continued, 'so, it was David Bowie, George Michael. People like that.'

She pictured the fairy lights in her childhood room, strung up across the wall above her vanity mirror. The small table the mirror stood on was practically hidden by a pile of books and a stereo. Its red power light was glowing, although the cassette inside had reached its end.

'George Michael could sing,' said the driver, nodding in approval. 'Do you know what my wife's favourite Christmas song is?'

'Oh wow!' said Alexis, her mind suddenly going blank. All she could think of was The Snowman, but she didn't think that was likely.

'Err, I don't know,' she said.

'Go on,' he pushed, 'guess!'

Suddenly the obvious answer sprung into her mind.

'Got it! Last Christmas!' she said confidently.

'No, it's Fairy tale of New York,' he said flatly, screwing up his face in disgust.

'What?' Alexis blurted out. 'That's rubbish!'

'I couldn't agree more,' he laughed.

Alexis laughed too, relieved that she hadn't inadvertently put her foot in her mouth.

He continued, 'But every year she insists on playing it and telling me it's her favourite.'

'Does she know you don't like it?'

'My dear, I've been married for almost forty years,' he said. 'That doesn't happen without knowing when to say what you really think, and when to just smile and nod.'

'Ha,' laughed Alexis, 'happy wife, happy life, right?'

'Exactly!' he replied, with a nod.

Just then, the familiar opening notes of "Club Tropicana" pulsed from the speakers.

'Hey!' shouted the driver. 'It's Georgie boy!'

His excited shouts jolted Tanya back into the present, a confused and fatigued look painted over her features.

'Shall I turn it up?' he asked, before noticing Tanya in his mirror. 'Oh, sorry love.'

'The volume's fine,' said Alexis reassuringly.

Tanya slumped back in her seat and returned

her eyes to the off position. Alexis also closed her eyes, but her ears were fully open, letting the song's rhythm and melody ride in like a surfer on the tide. She imagined a tropical environment. The ocean waves gently lapping against the shore. Vast, deep jungles spreading beyond the warm white sands. Somewhere a small waterfall splashed majestically onto a lagoon enticing any would be passers-by to dive into its cooling waters. Tom Hanks, the one from Joe vs the Volcano, not Cast Away, was running with a red Hawaiian garland around his neck. The scene was like a Bounty commercial, with Alexis as its star. She was in-between takes, stretched out on a lounger, wearing a red bikini, sipping on a martini. Looking out at the gorgeous sun in the early stages of setting, a tune about goldfish shores nibbling on her toes drifted on the salty air.

'Which number is it love?' asked the driver, snapping Alexis out of her happy place.

'Anywhere there on the left is fine thank you,' she said politely.

Alexis took care of the fee and both women got out.

'Shall I wait until you're indoors love?' asked the driver.

Alexis smiled.

'No, honestly, it's fine. Thank you.'

'Ok then. Take care now. Bye, bye.'

The taxi pulled away, turning at the end of the street and into the night in search of its next passenger.

7

'I'm sorry,' said Tanya quietly, standing by her front door.

Alexis had walked with Tanya to her house, even though it was past her own. They had been neighbours on the same street for about two years without even realising it.

Alexis had lived at number 54, but a piping problem turned out to be neither simple to fix, or as cheap, as her landlord, Mr Singh, had hoped. For a time, he complained to Alexis about this often, and loudly, though his frustrations were by no means aimed at her. She recognised the tone of a man often criticised at home, who simply needed the chance to air his own grievances. Ultimately, her understanding paid off. Recognising that it was unreasonable to expect Alexis to live there while the work was undertaken, they agreed that she would move into another of his properties. It was a win-win for them both, as his tenant would not be pressuring him to get the works done quickly (Mrs Singh was another matter), and Alexis would get a slightly bigger property for the same rent.

Alexis dealt with the move to number 37 in much the same way as she negotiated most things in life, rolling with things as they happened, just like shifting gears. While others would be losing it, Alexis could carry on, from the outside at least, unruffled, a trait that appealed to both Bobbi and Tanya, for different reasons.

She met them both, Bobbi first, through her online business, where she sold bespoke handmade items. A friend at work had passed on Alexis' website details, when Bobbi finally decided to start scrapbooking Louise's baby stuff, something she'd managed to put off for longer than expected, given her mum's persistent reminders. In truth, she lacked both the skill, and inclination to do it, but Jan insisted she should.

'She's growing up so fast, isn't she?' said Jan.

'Yes, I know,' said Bobbi. 'Her mouth is getting smarter every day.'

'She's a darling,' said Jan, taking a sip out of her "World's Best Grandmother" mug.

'She never shuts up you know?' said Bobbi. 'There isn't a minute in the day when she hasn't got something to say. I have to remind her to take a breath sometimes.'

'She's lovely,' cooed Jan. 'Those dresses won't fit her before long. Shall we have a look to the centre at the weekend?'

'Yes, more money.'

'Bobbi!' Jan scolded.

'It's true,' Bobbi protested.

'Yes, but you should enjoy these days.'

Bobbi sipped her tea.

'I see her every day you know. I've got no choice,' she said, half-exasperated, before laughing. 'But I know what you're going to say.' Putting on an old woman's voice, she said 'One day she'll be all grown up and you'll wonder, "Where did my little girl go?"'

Jan managed to stifle a smirk, raising her eyebrow in trying to look stern.

'Well Miss Clever Clogs! That may be true, but you'll also be wondering why your purse is always empty? You know...school uniform, phones, make-up (counting each on her fingers). It all costs.'

Bobbi finished her tea with a gulp.

'So, I should get that scrapbook done so I can sit one day with a glass of wine and remind myself of the good old days, right? Think back to a time when I was sleep deprived, and had a bit more money than I do now?'

Jan nodded.

'At least I can enjoy the fact that I was young once,' said Bobbi glumly.

'Yes,' Jan nodded, 'although you're not exactly young now, darling.'

'Cheeky cow!' laughed Bobbi.

Jan stuck her tongue out and made a mental note of her joke. She'd enjoy telling the girls that one at the Bingo halls later in the week.

'I can do it if you're too busy,' she offered. 'I know that you're-'

'No, no!' Bobbi interrupted. 'I'll do it. I know someone who has the stuff I need. Or at least she'll tell me what I need.'

'Who is she?' asked Jan.

'Alex, Alexa?' said Bobbi, searching her memory for the stranger's name. 'Emma at work told me about her.'

'I can't play any songs about Emma at work,' said Bobbi's Alexa device, bursting into life and giving them both a shock.

'Bloody thing,' laughed Bobbi. 'Just wait,' she said, raising her hand and gesturing to her mum, 'she'll forget about it in a sec.'

The light on the device dimmed.

'They're always listening, those things,' whispered Jan. 'That's what Sharon's husband is always saying anyway.'

'Anyway…' said Bobbi, shaking her head, 'Emma said that Al…err, that woman, is good. She would know because she likes all that kind of cra, err, cherished…memory making.'

Bobbi tried to cover up her verbal slip with an exaggerated smile.

'Have you got her number?' asked Jan. 'I'll have a look and see what she's got.'

'She's got a website. I'll send you a link later.'

Jan waved her hand.

'No, get me a number please darling, I don't know what links are!'

When Bobbi followed up and contacted Alexis, she liked her instantly. She passed on her details to Tanya too, having made plans to go for a cake and coffee in town and discovering that the two lived near one another.

Alexis was too tired to start going over what had happened earlier.

'It's ok,' she said from the gate. 'Get some rest

and we'll talk soon, ok?'

Tanya nodded and went indoors.

As she walked home, Alexis' thoughts were with Bobbi. Two calls went unanswered, and although slightly concerned, she knew Bobbi could take care of herself well enough for one night.

She was greeted at home by a cry from her cat, Twix.

'Hi baby!' she called.

She flicked the hallway light on and headed for the kitchen. The fluorescent strip light had been playing up, taking half a minute to blink into life, so she didn't bother turning it on, making do with the light behind her. It was probably something she could fix herself, but Mr Singh had insisted that he deal with all repairs, no matter how minor. She mentally noted to call him tomorrow and headed for the fridge.

When the light was on and the blind was up at night, as it was now, it had the effect of illuminating the whole room, like a museum installation, to any passer-by outside, either in the property's small garden or the path beyond. However, the observation was only one-way, a feeling Alexis found uncomfortable, so not wanting to be on display at this late hour, the gloom suited her. She trusted Twix would soon find her, which he duly did, coiling his furry tail around her leg. She put down a plate of food, which he happily tucked into, and then poured herself a glass of filtered water.

Taking a sip, Alexis lingered on her reflection in the kitchen window. She didn't suffer from vanity's often cruel taunts, accepting what she had been given, which wasn't, in her own opinion, unattractive by any means. She made an appreciation of her reflected face and form, tilting her head and arching her brows. She took another drink, a longer one. The chill of the liquid revitalised her somewhat, stripping away some of the self-flattery that the alcohol she had drunk provided.

She thought of the women she'd spent time with tonight and their relative beauty. How they tried to express it, through makeup, clothing etc. and how it revealed itself and changed in different environments. The glowing warmth of the restaurant and their facial twitches, provoked by animated discussion; the frantic movements of light on the dancefloor, casting their faces, and bodies, in varying combinations of light and dark, angle and shade; the cracks that had appeared from laughter, and then anger.

Even Lucy, with her youth and energy, was not impervious. It was certainly easy to claim that she was eye-catchingly beautiful, but it was a brittle beauty, as evidenced by her terrified expression at the end of the night. The argument between Bobbi and Tanya had rapidly transformed her from a young, enchanting woman to an anxious frightened girl. Alexis looked closer at her reflection, noticing how her eyes looked dark and tired.

Twix leapt onto the kitchen table, having finished his meal. She joined him and lowered her head. He seized on the implied invitation, slinking towards her, and rubbing her nose with his in appreciation. She kissed the top of his head and made her way upstairs to bed.

'Hi, I'm Lucy. I'm here for the spinning class at twenty past seven.'

The attendant took Lucy's fob unenthusiastically and scanned it on the sensor next to her screen. Glancing at the pixelated image that popped up only dismayed her further as the being in front of her was not only pretty in person, but photogenic too. The woman, who was twenty years older and about twenty pounds heavier than Lucy, handed the device back and signalled to the desk.

'Sign in please,' she grunted, forcing her features into a smile.

Lucy obliged before striding through the reception area and turning left towards the changing rooms. She was familiar with locker room environments having represented her school and college playing netball. She gave up the game at university but found other activities to enjoy on campus including swimming, tennis and running. The constant training was hard work, but she loved it, plus she looked amazing. She was proud of her appearance, not in a narcissistic way, but just the good vibes you get when you know you're looking after yourself. She had been willing to work hard and appearing healthy was her reward for that effort. If being twenty-one wasn't enough of a gift, with a bounty of natural energy and charm to draw on, the bonus of a toned petite body to power her through life was the delightful cherry on top of a particularly beautiful cake.

However, being in a locker room surrounded by her peers was completely different to what she experienced at the first leisure centre she visited. The centre was small for a start, with a limited number of classes, although the gym was of a reasonable size compared to the rest of the site. She spent of a couple of weeks there, hoping to buddy up with another woman, but unfortunately, found it was used predominately by men. That didn't bother her, and the feeling was mutual as the guys would cast subtle, and sometimes not so subtle, glances her way. Unfortunately, most of the female members tended to visit during the day when Lucy was at work, while the few she did manage to speak to weren't as friendly as she hoped they might be. Unperturbed, she found another gym, which had more classes, including spinning, which she was yet to try.

After university, Lucy moved back home. The city was close enough that she could still enjoy a visit now and then, but it was too far away to use the facilities there as frequently as she wanted to. Many of her friends could think of nothing worse than being back at home, but it was a sensible choice, and truthfully, Lucy enjoyed being there, almost as much as her mum enjoyed having her baby back.

Now graduation was wrapped up, she'd discussed her options with her parents, who encouraged her to find a temporary job. They didn't want her to pay rent, but knew it was important for

Lucy to have her own money, something she'd earned, until she figured out what she wanted to do and work on securing a more permanent role. Her parents had been smart with their money, buying their home early and managing debt well. Her dad wanted Lucy to have the same pride in owning her own place someday, seeing renting as throwing money away. He had also become accustomed to having easy access to the bathroom. He enjoyed being able to take his time on the toilet, where he could catch up on the latest news on his phone, and so he looked forward to having that freedom again someday.

Most of all though, her mum and dad wanted Lucy to have some fun. After all, she'd worked hard for her degree, and she deserved some time to let her hair down. Her mum always said that her twenties were the best years of her life and naturally, she wanted the same for her daughter. Both of her parents had travelled at that time in their lives and met shortly afterwards.

'Any idiot can sow an oat,' her mum once said, 'but you need to know what crops you like best. The only way you can find out what you like is by going to the market and seeing what's on offer.'

Lucy was eleven when her mum gave her this advice. Around this time, she'd had 'sex education' classes at school. When her dad saw the leaflet from school, he remembered there was something he had to buy from the shops and directed Lucy to her mum to have a chat.

'The important thing,' said her mum, continuing with her metaphor, 'is not to waste your money on someone who's not worthy. Don't just open your purse to anyone.'

Lucy looked puzzled.

'My purse?' she asked.

Her mum pointed between Lucy's legs.

'Mum!' shrieked Lucy, as her mum erupted with laughter.

Lucy's grandmother was walking by.

'What's all this noise going on in here?' she asked.

'It's mum,' said Lucy, pointing at her, 'she's being rude.'

'What do you mean child?' beckoning her granddaughter to come as she sat in her chair.

Lucy sat on the chair arm and put her arm around her grandmother.

'Tell grandma what you just said.'

Lucy's mum repeated her advice, to which her grandma nodded.

'She's right,' she said firmly.

She looked at her granddaughter, lifting her hand and gently shaping it around her cheek.

'You only have yourself to blame if you go shopping for a banana and come home with a shrivelled runner bean and a couple of nuts.'

'Grandma!' screamed Lucy. 'Oh my god!' she cried, jumping up and lifting her hands to cover her eyes.

The women were in stitches. All words

escaped Lucy's mind, as blood flushed her cheeks. She left the room for a moment, before returning with a drink, shaking her head at the two women who were now reading the school note.

They asked what she'd been told at school and Lucy said they'd watched an animated video where the man and woman were holding hands, and then kissed. The teacher paused the video when both the man and woman were shown side by side, naked. She said they looked like a drawing in her biology textbook, with labels and arrows pointing to their different bits and bobs.

'Can you remember some of the names?' her mum asked.

'The man had his penis, and a scroat, scrotum?' she said, slightly embarrassed.

'Scrotum, yes,' her mum confirmed.

Grandma giggled beside her.

'The woman had a vagina, and tubes,' said Lucy. 'There was more but I can't remember.'

'Vulva? Clitoris?' her mum suggested.

'Yes, vulva. I don't think the other one was there though,' said Lucy.

'Must have been drawn by a man,' said her grandma.

Lucy's mum tried her best not to laugh, but quickly gave in. Lucy looked at them both, a bemused smile on her face.

'Why are you laughing?' she asked, chuckling herself as their good mood infected her.

'Ask your father when he gets back,' said

grandma.

'Ma!' shouted Lucy's mum, slapping the old woman on the arm, before breaking into laughs again. The women, and Lucy, all laughed so much they cried.

Eventually, their sides aching, normal service resumed with mum pouring the tea, Lucy making toast, and grandma settling herself in her chair ready for an episode of Countdown. By the time Lucy's dad came home, a few hours later, she'd finished her homework and had fallen asleep watching TV in her room. He kissed her on the brow and turned off the TV and light, having unknowingly dodged a bullet.

9

'I'm sorry,' said the tall woman, 'but my friend is using that one,' gesturing at Lucy.

It had been three months since Lucy had started working at "Daintily Does It" on a temporary contract to cover a period of maternity leave. The pay wasn't great, but the job was fine being close to home and not too demanding. She enjoyed chatting to customers on the phone in her easy manner, hearing about their projects, and suggesting products they might find useful. At times, it didn't really feel like work and so afterwards, Lucy could keep up with being active. She'd arrived at the gym a little earlier that day than necessary, so as not to be late for the class.

Getting up so early had been a bit of a struggle, given that she was enjoying the comforts of being at home, but there had been spells at university when Lucy would get up at 6am and be pounding the streets by 6.15 for a morning jog. She liked how the familiar streets and venues she'd see going to and from classes, could look so alien so soon after dawn, when the light and temperature was decidedly cooler. On her runs, the soundtrack of birds, and sleepy retailers lifting shop shutters, was so much clearer without the toxic drone of vehicle engines shouting over everything. By the time she'd get back to her digs, the air would be percolated, with the sun lazily rising, like warmed up coffee. Lucy would pour herself a

cup, ready for the day ahead.
She half expected the class to be quiet but was surprised to see so many names on the signing in sheet. The changing room was busy, with more ladies already busily chatting outside the exercise room. When they entered, Lucy noticed a woman, talking to a man at the back of the room who she rightly guessed was the class instructor. They shook hands before he made his way to the front of the class. The woman was tall and despite being older than Lucy, her skin had a youthful glow, which made it difficult to guess how old she may have been. Another woman had reached the spare bike next to her before Lucy, but was happy to move, taking a free station in the row ahead. Lucy smiled and climbed onto the bike.

'Thank you,' she beamed. 'I'm Lucy,' she said, extending her hand.

'Claire,' replied the woman.

Claire shook Lucy's hand with a firm, but friendly, grip.

'Have you done this type of class before?'

'No, it's my first time. Have you?'

'Yes, but you look like you're going to do great. I'll do my best to keep up with you.'

Lucy smiled as she got into position, placing her water bottle in the holder. The bike was uncomfortable, partly due to the seat being left in a high position from its last occupant. Claire watched as Lucy figured out how to readjust the device, resisting the temptation to intervene. She nodded her approval when Lucy flashed her a smile having finally settled.

It turned out that not only did Claire look in great shape, but she *was* in fantastic shape. The first ten minutes were fine before Lucy hit the proverbial brick wall. She recovered half-way through, gaining a second wind, but wished she had been more sensible and chosen the thirty rather than forty-minute class, for her first time. By the end, she was exhausted but elated. Beside her, Claire was equally spent, but had a huge smile on her face.

'Wow, that was fantastic!' said Lucy, catching her breath. 'How long have you been training?'

'Since I was at school,' said Claire, taking a drink. 'I've always loved being active. Do you swim?'

'Not so much now I'm back home,' said Lucy, 'but I did a lot when I was at university.'

'Other sports too?'

'Yes, I love it.'

'They've got a good pool here,' said Claire, gesturing to the other side of the complex. 'I like the gym mostly, but it's great after a session to just sit in the jacuzzi and steam room. Tuesday nights are usually the best time, quietest.'

'Cool!' said Lucy. 'I haven't been in one before actually. Not sure how comfortable I'd be with that.'

'How'd you mean?' asked Claire.

'Well, you know. Don't you have to be naked?' Lucy asked awkwardly.

Claire stared at Lucy.

'Yes, have you got a problem with that?' her tone low and firm.

'I, well no,' stuttered Lucy, 'I mean, I-'

'Lucy, I'm fucking with you!' said Claire, with a wide smile.

Lucy laughed.

'Oh' she said.

She was slightly shocked to hear a grown up swear, but she liked it as it made her feel like a grown up too. Her parents never swore around her, although she had heard her mum say 'shit' once or twice, usually after dropping something or muttering to herself after being on the phone to Lucy's dad.

Lucy playfully slapped her brow.

'What an idiot! I don't know why I thought that.'

'I mean, you can if you want,' said Claire, 'but you might get a few funny looks if anyone else was in there with you. I mean the women of course. I'm sure the guys wouldn't mind at all.'

'Oh, it's shared! Well, I'm glad you told me.'

The two women laughed as they talked through such a scenario.

Lucy showered and was pleased to see that Claire had waited in the reception area for her so they could exchange numbers. The class was repeated three times a week, so as they parted, they shook hands having agreed to meet again at the next one. Lucy headed off to work, buzzing with excitement from the workout and from meeting Claire.

'Did you not see me?' asked Bobbi.

She was sitting by the window, looking out at the traffic by the roundabout opposite her work when the sudden ping of the microwave brought her back into the room. The scent of something delicious caused her head to turn, which is when she saw Tanya heading toward the exit. She called, beckoning her to come over. For the slightest of moments, Tanya seemed to pause, as if she was contemplating just carrying on in the direction she was heading. However, judging that it wasn't plausible to say she hadn't heard Bobbi, she pivoted.

'I did,' she said as she approached Bobbi, 'but you seemed like you were away with your thoughts, so I was just going to head back to the office.'

Bobbi waved away Tanya's reasoning.

'Oh no, it's nothing. That smells nice. What is it?'

Tanya sat opposite Bobbi and unrolled her cutlery from a napkin, while Bobbi inspected her food. Her Tupperware tray contained a curry of some description, either Indian or Chinese.

'It's tofu and black bean sauce, with rice, obviously,' she said, poking the grains with her fork. 'Just leftovers from last night.'

'Ooh lovely,' said Bobbi. 'That's the tofu, is it?' pointing at a white lump in the tray, glazed with the sticky sauce.

'Yes. Have you tried it?'

'Err, no. Mike would wonder what the hell I was serving him if I gave him that.'

'Really? I thought he was vegetarian before.'

'Well,' Bobbi mused, 'I think he kinda, sorta, dabbled with it when he was younger. Said he wasn't going to eat meat, except for a bacon sarnie on a Saturday, that kind of thing. He sometimes buys those vegetarian sausages though from Linda Wotsit.'

'He'd probably like it,' said Tanya. 'It doesn't taste of much really on its own though.'

'How do you cook it?' asked Bobbi.

'It's easy. You just drain it, press it for a while, and then-'

'I'll stop you there,' said Bobbi, holding up her hand, 'sounds like too much of a faff.'

'Well,' said Tanya, 'you do what you want!'

Bobbi raised her eyebrow at Tanya's curt tone. Tanya stabbed a lump and some rice and lifted the fork to her mouth.

'How was your meeting?' asked Bobbi. It was this morning, right?'

'It's this afternoon. I'm not looking forward to it,' said Tanya.

'Why, what's up?'

Tanya let out a little sigh.

'It's just a waste of time. It's a bunch of guys, making stupid jokes for forty-five minutes, and then they'll squeeze, like ten minutes in at the end to talk about the meeting.'

'Who's that?' asked Bobbi. 'Paul, John?'

'Yeah,' nodded Tanya. 'Andrew, and Joan from

Finance. All that lot.'

'Aren't Anne, and Florence there too?'

'Yes. Anne doesn't say much, really. But Florence is just as bad as them. She's always talking about where she was drinking at the weekend. In almost all her stories, she's either got a drink in her hand, or she's got a hangover.'

'Ha-ha, bloody hell!' laughed Bobbi.

'You'd think she'd know better at her age,' said Tanya, sounding irritated.

'What do you mean at her age?' said Bobbi, taken aback. 'She's only, what…err, two years older than me?'

'Yes, but you're not out every weekend, are you?' countered Tanya.

'I doubt she's out every weekend.'

'You'd think so the way she goes on.'

'Well, I'm sure as hell not,' said Bobbi. 'Me and him have a drink in the house on a Friday night, and I'll have a glass or two during the week, but that's it.'

Tanya tried to speak with a mouthful of rice. 'How often?' she mumbled.

'How often? Probably two, three nights a week,' guessed Bobbi.

'Sounds like you and Florence would get on well.'

'Hey,' Bobbi blurted out, 'it's hard when you've got…'

She paused.

Tanya looked at her before looking back down at her food.

'You can say it you know. Just because I don't want them, doesn't mean I deny they exist.'

Bobbi studied Tanya's face.

'Yes, it is hard when you've got kids. And I only have one. Spare a thought for those poor sods who have more than one to deal with.'

'Their choice,' shrugged Tanya. 'If they didn't want any more, they should have kept their legs closed.'

Bobbi put down her sandwich.

'Ok, what's going on?

'What?' said Tanya, looking at Bobbi blankly.

'You're in a snipy mood.'

Tanya shook her head.

'It's just that meeting.'

'How's your dad?' asked Bobbi, trying a different tact. 'Has there been any interest yet?'

'Yes, actually,' said Tanya quietly.

'Really? Well, that's great. It's only been on the market, what, five minutes?'

'I know,' said Tanya, pushing her food around. 'There was a lot of interest. He had a few people viewing it last weekend, one offered a little over the asking price, and he accepted.'

'Wow! That is fast.'

Bobbi's statement hung in the air as Tanya showed no sign of responding.

'Well, tell him congratulations from me.'

'Thanks,' said Tanya, half-heartedly.

'It'll be a weight off his mind, I'm sure' said Bobbi. 'So, it's all systems go with the move then?'

Tanya sighed again.

'Yes. He can't wait' she said.

'It's great news, Tanya. It really is.'

'If you say so,' she shrugged.

'And look, try not to get stressed out about this meeting. Maybe you should try to be more like Anne.'

Tanya looked at Bobbi with a dead stare.

'I know,' said Bobbi, wiping her mouth, 'they're not words I thought I'd ever hear myself say. But it sounds like she just lets it all go over her head.'

Tanya scrunched her nose up.

'Hmm. What's option B?'

'Option B, is, maybe you should, you know…?'

'What?'

Bobbi bit into her sandwich. In a muffled voice, she said: 'Maybe you should join in too.'

'You're kidding?' said Tanya, sitting upright.

'Why not? You can be funny.'

Tanya lolled her head from side to side, as if she was thinking about Bobbi's suggestion.

'Yeah, I don't want to. Besides, I haven't got anything in common with these people.'

Bobbi leaned closer to Tanya.

'Look,' she said in a softer voice, 'I'm not saying you have to be best friends with them. Just, sometimes try and laugh along.'

Tanya shook her head.

'I don't think that's going to happen, Bobbi.'

Tanya made a show of checking her watch, before wiping her mouth, and placing the napkin and cutlery in the tub, snapping the lid closed.

'I have to get going. I need to prep a few things before it starts.'

'Ok,' said Bobbi, popping the last bite of sandwich in her mouth as they stood up together. 'Oh, just quickly' she said, trying to swallow fast, 'in a few weeks I'm going to be home alone. Mike's taking Lou to his mum's.'

'Why aren't you going?'

'Caravans aren't for me really. Anyway, I was thinking it would be a perfect chance for a night out. I thought I'd ask that new girl, Lucy. You've seen her right?'

Tanya started to slowly drift towards the exit, attempting to wind the conversation up.

'She's a bit young, isn't she?'

'Well yeah, she's twenty-one, but she's lovely. It'll be great. I was thinking four, no three weeks on Friday. Bit of food, a few drinks, some dancing. You'll come, right?'

'I'll let you know,' said Tanya, unenthusiastically.

'It'll be a laugh, honest. Just the thing to cheer you up.'

Tanya sighed for a third time.

'I don't need cheering up.'

'You know what I mean,' Bobbi pleaded.

The two women parted with a wave and headed to their offices, Bobbi's on the second floor and Tanya's towards the far end, behind the shop floor. Bobbi felt so excited about the night out, forgoing the lift, and instead, choosing the stairs. Tanya tried to think about what she had to prepare for the meeting but couldn't shake off Bobbi's last comment.

11

'1km to go,' she thought.

The jog at the end of a workout session was Claire's favourite part of gym night. That said, she certainly enjoyed the weight machines too, for the effort it took to stay focused when using them. Over time she'd become dedicated to building a body for herself that was strong, so avoiding harm through poor form was essential. On her first session, back in her college days, she decided to have a trainer. He instilled in her the importance of maximising each motion.

'Engage the muscle' he would say.

She loved that concept, the idea of having a conversation you could say, with the inner network of strength, muscles, tendons, fibres etc. on which she so depended. It became like a personal type of yoga or meditation for Claire, something unique that she had taught herself by listening to and learning from her body. In front of a mirror, she would move, bend, twist, sway, turn, flex, lift, stretch, roll, contract, and relax her limbs, marvelling at how it all connected and worked together so fluidly. The ability to move, a gift really, never ceased to amaze Claire, so grateful she was for the incredible tool she'd been given.

She'd always had dips of course, like everyone does. Times when she was less motivated or had let situations get the better of her. When that happened, inevitably her training suffered, but the impact of those situations would always be just a temporary blip. Claire would quickly realise the benefits she was missing out on and would prioritise her activity accordingly to get herself back on track.

From an early age, Claire recognised that she was selfishly inclined to put her own needs first. Despite the barrage of voices that challenged and condemned such an attitude, she resisted the pressure of peer and social conformity, and embraced her inclination. Far from being a negative thing, Claire reasoned that if she was strong, pursued what she wanted to do, was 'happy' if you like, then others would benefit from her strength, her output, and her joy.

It didn't always work out that way of course, as a failed marriage would attest, but even that disaster gave her the gift of her son, Jonathan, who was now ten. Claire was self-aware enough too to recognise when she'd made mistakes. There was plenty she could lay at Bill's door, and nobody would have argued with her for that, but she knew there were many times, when she could have said, or done, things a little better.

These moments of introspection tended to happen when she ran, as she was now, closing in on a casual 5km to wrap up another successful session.

She thought about a time at primary school, playing hopscotch with a friend called Kelly. They took it in turns, tossing a pebble to land on the chalk drawn numbers and hopping through the grid, trying to keep balanced without treading on the lines. A boy called Toby, who tended to snatch and grab things without asking, was running around the yard. He saw the girls playing, and in his immature mind, thought it would be hilarious to ruin their game. He ran over and stood to the side. Kelly started her turn. The stone landed on seven, and she began to hop. As she bent down on one leg to pick up the stone, Toby, who was bigger than Kelly, pushed her over. Enraged, Claire, who was taller than most of the kids in her class, including Toby, shoved him to the ground. She stood over him, as he stared up at her in a state of shock, pain shooting from his backside where it had connected with concrete.

Before his lip started to quiver, he scrambled to his feet and shouted, 'I'm telling,' before running off. Claire turned and helped Kelly up, who was limping slightly.

'Don't let him push you again, ok?' said Claire.

'I didn't see him,' sobbed Kelly.

'Stop crying. Next time you see him, you push him.'

It probably wasn't the best advice to give, but she was only six at the time, and Kelly never followed it anyway. Thinking about it now, it was a confirmation of a truth that Claire had heard in the echoes of her memories, narrated by her grandfather, many times throughout her life, namely:

'If you're big enough to give it, you have to be big enough to take it too.'

Toby from that point on would frown whenever his eyes met Claire's, right up until they went off to different 'big' schools. Their paths never crossed again.

'So, I'm sorry this is short notice, but I'm going out with some friends on Friday, and I wondered if you'd like to come along?' asked Lucy.

After finishing their work in the gym, the pair had agreed to meet in the on-site café for a coffee and chat. Claire was slightly surprised by Lucy's offer and thought about her options for tomorrow night as she lingered on the latte she was sipping. Truthfully, she was genuinely flattered to be asked, and wanted to say yes. It was easy to enjoy Lucy's bright and easy company. Her youthful innocence, you could say, was almost entirely intact, with a personality that shone, not hidden behind layers of defensiveness, cynicism, or bitterness, which Claire typically experienced with other women.

'Do you mean tomorrow?' she asked.

Lucy nodded.

'Well, I dropped Jonathan off at his dads for the weekend earlier so, yeah, that should be fine. Are you sure your friends won't mind an older bird like me tagging along?'

'No,' said Lucy, 'actually it's with some friends at work and they're all as old as you.'

Claire chuckled.

Lucy, realising what she had said tried to recover.

'Sorry, I meant older, like you. I'll be the youngest one there basically,' she gabbled, feeling herself starting to sweat a little.

'Ha, it's lucky you're pretty,' said Claire, laughing.

'Sorry,' said Lucy, blushing slightly.

'No, don't worry about it. Who else is going then?'

'Bobbi asked me,' said Lucy. 'She's really nice. When I started at work, she was one of the people that did the induction thing they had. I've met her for lunch a few times. She cracks me up, so I think you'll like her.'

'Is it her birthday or something?' asked Claire.

'No, nothing like that. She said her husband, she's married, was away with her daughter, and so she just fancied a night out.'

'Amen to that. Who else?'

'Erm, well Bobbi said she'd asked her friend Tanya. She hadn't said yes yet, but she thought she would.'

'Do you know her too?' asked Claire, taking another sip of her drink.

'I've seen her once or twice, with Bobbi. She seems a little surly, like she doesn't smile a lot. I'm sure she's lovely though. Bobbi said Alexis is coming too. She doesn't work with us though.'

'What does she do?'

'I'm not sure, I haven't met her before.'

'It's ok, I can ask her myself,' said Claire with a smile.

'You're going to come then?' asked Lucy, her face lighting up.

'Yes. Thank you for asking me.'

Lucy clapped with excitement and launched into a giddy exploration of what she and Claire might wear. Claire suggested that Lucy could get ready and stay at her place, so they could share a taxi, and she'd drop her back home the next day, an offer Lucy accepted happily.

'It wasn't like you at all,' said Alexis.

'No, I know that,' said Bobbi.

Alexis had arrived bang on 12pm as she had indicated. She'd brought cookies, a mix of white and chocolate chip, which she'd bought yesterday at lunchtime, thinking ahead of time. She knew that she would likely visit Bobbi the morning after, just to check in and have a laugh about the night's events. The cookies were intended as a treat, to help nurse a sore head after alcohol. She didn't anticipate that they would be needed as part of a makeshift counselling session.

Bobbi sat holding the cup of tea Alexis had made with some effort, her head aching still. She was shaped like a ball on the couch, her legs tucked underneath her body. With her large hoodie and sweatpants, she had dressed like someone who had pushed themselves to get ready while their body protested the whole time. She'd showered, and her hair was still slightly damp in places, tied back in a bun. Her face was a little pale, but her eyes did not look quite as puffy as they felt in Bobbi's head. Apart from feeling a little tired, Alexis was her usual, perfectly presentable self.

'At the same time, I do understand why you were frustrated last night. I mean, I haven't really spent that much time with Tanya. We,' pointing at Bobbi and then herself, 'have known each other longer obviously, and spent a lot more time together.

And…it's not like I haven't tried to get to know, Tanya. I've invited her round for coffee or asked her to come along when I've popped into town, or what have you. She'll say yes, but then nothing comes off it.'

Bobbi nodded.

'When that happens once or twice, you think, ok, maybe this or that happened. Whatever, you can let it go. After that though, I think it's fine if you decide to stop asking. At some point you just think "Well, you know, it's up to them". There's no sense in chasing someone is there? I've got enough to do, Bobbi, with my business, and whatever else.'

'She's not easy to get to know,' said Bobbi. 'I mean, I met her back at college. Things were different then. Hell, how long ago is that…fourteen years? It's like a different life.'

'What was she like back then?' asked Alexis, sipping her tea.

'Not too dissimilar really. She was still quiet, well, shy more like. I wasn't quite so much of a gobshite, back then. But we got paired up in an assignment. She was good at the work, like she seemed to know what she was doing, and so we just kind of went from there. We haven't always worked together. At the same place, I mean.'

'Yeah,' nodded Alexis, 'she mentioned, you'd worked there for three years?'

'Yes, well, I had Lou Lou when I was twenty-seven, and didn't work for the first two years. We were lucky to have two sets of grandparents to call on. Well, I mean my mum, and Mike's mum. My dad died when I was twenty-five, and Mike's when he was just a boy.'

'I'm sorry, Bobbi. I don't think I've asked you before about your dad. I didn't know it was that recent.'

Bobbi waved her hand.

'No, don't worry. I mean it's not really, it's what...I'm thirty-four, so nine years. Yeah, what month are we in now?'

'June,' said Alexis.

'Right, so yeah, nine years in August. It is what it is.'

Bobbi took a sip of her tea, which Alexis mimicked, before continuing. 'He ate a lot of, let's say 'not particularly healthy' stuff, and had a heart attack when he was 49. I think there were other factors, but basically, that was it.'

'Oh God! That's awful!'

'Thank you. I don't think my mum has forgiven him, but that's another story for another time.'

Alexis took another sip of tea, while Bobbi picked out a cookie. They had hardened overnight ever so slightly but were still malleable.

'Anyway, so yeah, three years I've been working there. Tanya had already been there for six months. She told me about the job when it was advertised.'

'Did you mean all those things you said last night? About Tanya, I mean?' asked Alexis.

Bobbi rubbed her brow.

'Yeah, to be honest, I don't remember everything I said. So, I may have gone a little overboard. I don't know. I remember you telling me to stop.'

Alexis thought she might be called on to fill in the gaps, and so spoke her words slowly and deliberately with consideration.

'The thing is, it was late…it was the end of the night, everyone was a bit tired, everyone's had a few drinks, so mouths are a little, looser…and I was just worried that somebody was going to say, or do, something that they regretted.'

'And I do,' said Bobbi. 'I feel bad about it, I mean.'

'Tanya was out of order. Not to sound childish, but you could say she started it,' Alexis said pointedly.

'All night, Alexis!' Bobbi said hurriedly. 'She was in a foul mood, from the moment I met up with her at The Watering Hole. Did you notice that something was a little off about her?'

'Well, I saw you first, at the bar. I didn't see Tanya until you pointed her out because she was just kind of, closed off from the rest of the room.'

'I don't know if you noticed,' said Bobbi, 'but she was like that all night too. Just snipy, moody, not enjoying herself. Not even trying to enjoy herself. I felt quite embarrassed for Lucy, poor kid. She'd invited Claire to have a good time and then all this happens.'

Bobbi puffed out her cheeks. She undid her bobble, so she could run her fingers through her hair.

'I spoke to Lucy this morning,' said Alexis.

'Is she ok?' asked Bobbi.

Alexis nodded.

'She's fine. She stayed at Claire's, but I think that was prearranged.'

Bobbi nodded.

'When I spoke to her,' continued Alexis, 'Claire had just dropped her off, so she was going to go to bed for a little bit. I told her I was coming to see you, so she said to say "Hi".'

'Aww, that's nice,' Bobbi said, managing to raise a slight smile. 'She doesn't hate me then?'

'No, and I don't think Claire was bothered either. I know she's older, but she seemed like she can handle herself alright.'

'Well, I'm less concerned about Claire. I mean, I didn't know the woman until yesterday. Lucy's just a kid though, really.'

'Give her a call later,' suggested Alexis, wrinkling her nose.

'Yeah I will. When I've pulled myself together a bit more.'

Bobbi bit into the cookie. She stared at the crumbs, which had fallen onto her top, eating the largest and flicking two or three of the others off, before brushing whatever was left away to fall into the deep pile of the main rug.

Alexis looked at her, setting her cup down on the coffee table.

'Are you ok?' Alexis asked gently.

Bobbi sighed.

'Not really, Lexi. I feel very shitty,' she said, her voice coming close to cracking. She took a moment to compose herself.

'I mean, I'm so annoyed at her. I'm annoyed at myself too. I shouldn't have let her push my buttons like that. She has been going through some stuff, I'm not denying that, or belittling it at all, but she never asks about me, you know. I think she just thinks that I have Mike, or you, or my mum to talk to, and that's fine, so she doesn't need to ask how I'm doing.'

'Well, you do have all of those things?' said Alexis, a little blunter than she'd intended.

'I know that, but do you know what I mean?'

'I do, of course.'

'It isn't like me to blow up like that, at all. I'm usually so much more in control. God, I sound like I'm making excuses.'

Alexis shook her head.

'No, they're not excuses. You've told me about her last relationship, and she told me herself about her dad.'

'When did she tell you that?'

'Last night.'

'And what did she say?'

'She…misses him.'

'Yeah,' said Bobbi, almost inaudibly.

'It's understandable, really,' added Alexis.

'Yes,' countered Bobbi, 'but you have to move on from things, don't you?'

'This is true,' said Alexis.

She stood to take her cup to the kitchen. 'Are you finished with that?' she asked, gesturing at Bobbi's cup.

'You're ok,' said Bobbi, 'just leave yours on the side and I'll get another just now.'

Bobbi ran her fingers through her hair again. She heard Alexis rinse the cup out at the sink and place it on the rack. She dried her hands on a tea-towel before returning. She sat next to Bobbi and offered her arms for a hug, which Bobbi accepted, sinking into her embrace. Alexis leant back against the sofa's cushions with Bobbi's head resting on her chest, her arms loosely draped around her.

'You know,' said Bobbi, 'it's bad enough when you think negative things about yourself, but to hear someone else saying them is awful. Just hearing them out loud, sort of makes them feel more real.'

'What kind of things?' said Alexis, stroking Bobbi's hair.

Bobbi hesitated.

'Do you think I'm a bitch?'

Alexis gave a slight laugh.

'Oh no, of course you're not.'

For a few moments, they said nothing, although Bobbi sobbed a little. They sat on the couch, holding each other until Bobbi broke the silence.

'I'm not sure I can forgive her, Lexi. For what she said about them.'

'Who?' asked Alexis.

Bobbi nodded at a picture on the mantelpiece.

'Ah right, I remember,' said Alexis.

The picture contained a nearby park and was of the three of them, sitting on one of those giant swings you can lie down on. Each of them had huge smiles, forever fixed on their faces by the click of a button.

13

'Thank you!' said Bobbi, as was the custom, dropping her ticket into the labelled slot by the driver. She'd noticed on the ride in that, at each stop, he enthusiastically sent passengers on their way with a chirpy farewell. Others had noticed it too as they exchanged smirks with one another, and so Bobbi couldn't resist a smile when she received the same treatment.

Although happy, she resisted the urge to hop off the vehicle. Her shoes were nothing like those the younger women she saw totter around in, but having donned a small thick heel, the risk of an ungraceful stumble was enough of a deterrent. There was every chance the night would conspire to present an opportunity for her to make a tit of herself, so it made no sense trying to create her own before a drop of alcohol had even touched her lips.

Straightening her jacket and clutching her purse, Bobbi strode down the high street, feeling confident with a smile on her face, like someone appreciating a private joke. She'd missed just having a bit of time where she could be out and meet up with a few mates, not as Mike's wife, or Louise's mum, but just as Bobbi, out to enjoy a pint and have a laugh.

The Watering Hole was exactly Bobbi's kind of place. It was a no-nonsense kind of pub, with a long bar, a pool table and dart board, and a jukebox. It was the sort of place that had punters rather than clientele which other establishments fawned to attract. It was a bit rough here and there, as were the said punters, but with charm to spare it ticked Bobbi's boxes. There were small round tables, with stools for people to squat on like overgrown toddlers, and several booths, with comfortable but slightly worn leather seating. It reminded her of the bar in Cheers, with its very own Sam Malone in the form of Dave, its owner, chief barman, and piss taker extraordinaire. At this time in the evening, being at the top end of town, it was quiet, but later, it would be a different scene. Those waiting at the main taxi ranks a short distance away, wouldn't fail to hear alcoholic melodies drifting on the chilly air, as fantasy rock stars belted out songs they'd lived with as children and adults, from school discos to weddings.

Bobbi quickly spotted Tanya, sitting on a stool on the far side of the premises. She couldn't have been further away from the small groups dotted here and there if she'd tried, which she most likely did. Bobbi's excitement level spluttered momentarily, like an engine hit by a bird strike, on seeing Tanya's glum expression. Hoping to tap back into that happy state of mind, she mentally walked herself back to the bus and the driver's cheery chubby face. Absorbing a deep breathe, she forced a smile, and as if to over-compensate, let out an exaggerated 'Hiya' as she moved towards Tanya.

Tanya didn't see, or sense Bobbi's approach, until she was standing almost in front of her.

'Hi' she said, with little enthusiasm and

without looking up.

'You alright?' asked Bobbi uncertainly. The smile on her face remained intact but was becoming increasingly under duress.

'Yes,' Tanya said before looking up. 'Yes, sorry.'

She tucked the phone away into her purse and leaned forward without leaving her stool. Bobbi moved closer for a cool embrace.

'Have you been here long?'

Bobbi turned to scan the bar after asking, not wanting to become embroiled in whatever drama had appeared on Tanya's phone screen.

'Not really, but too long for that barman, I think.'

'Who, Dave? The one in the black shirt.'

'No, the younger one,' said Tanya, a hint of disdain in her voice.

'Oh, I don't know him,' said Bobbi. 'Maybe he's new? He looks like a student.'

'He's clearly not studying customer service,' Tanya tutted. 'It took him an age to serve me, and then he asked if I wanted ice. I mean, I'm drinking coke,' she said, lifting her glass, 'of course I want ice.'

Tanya paused for a reaction, which Bobbi was slow to provide.

'Anyway,' she continued, 'after another eternity, he comes back and says there's no ice. No apology either.'

'That's...shocking!' Bobbi said. 'I don't know what the world is coming to.'

'It's not even proper coke. It's that awful draft stuff,' said Tanya, ignoring Bobbi's sarcasm.

'Are you not drinking tonight?' asked Bobbi. 'Did you drive in?'

'No, I will. Just not yet.'

Tanya stirred her drink with a black straw. She took a sip and gurned in displeasure as the near flat liquid dripped down her throat.

'How's your dad?' asked Bobbi, changing the subject. 'Is he getting settled in now?'

'Yes, I think so,' said Tanya, her tone flat and emotionless. 'He's making a few friends, getting to know people round about. Finding some good walks. He was even talking about joining a spa.'

'Wow, really! That's great!' said Bobbi, trying to inject some energy into the conversation.

'Well, you know, it's more like a health place, with a gym, small pool etc. It looks good.'

Tanya paused momentarily, imagining the images on the spa's website, which he'd shared to ask her opinion.

'It'll do him good,' she surmised.

'It was a hard time all of that,' offered Bobbi. 'I know it was quick but selling up, downsizing; at the end of the day, we all want to retire sometime. It feels like a bloody eternity away some days, so he is lucky.'

Tanya looked at her sharply.

'No, not lucky,' Bobbi clarified, 'I mean, he's worked hard obviously. He deserves it.'

Tanya pulled her phone out again, her face frowning.

'I think I've got time for a drink before Alexis gets here,' said Bobbi hurriedly. 'Do you want anything?'

Tanya held her glass up to her face and forced a grin.

'No thanks, I think I'm good.'

Bobbi snorted a laugh and headed over to the bar.

The younger bartender was nowhere to be seen, while Dave was topping off the last pint for a customer. With a packet of crisps dangling from his mouth, she watched this guy nervously clamp three lagers together between his red fingers, before slowly heading over to his pals.

'Hey, we don't allow your type in here,' said Dave.

Bobbi swivelled back around.

'Is that right?' she asked with a smirk. 'And what type would that be?'

'Heel wearing…'

'Aha,' she smirked.

'…middle aged, cougars,' he said.

'Middle-aged? You cheeky bastard!' she cried, in mock offense. 'Are you working here as part of a "Care in the Community" scheme?'

'Yeah,' smirked Dave, 'B&Q had no vacancies. How's Mike and the sprog?'

'They're great, thanks.'

'So, what are you doing here?' he asked.

'Hoping to get a drink if the barman can get his arse in gear,' she said.

'Ha-ha, no worries there. Letting your hair down tonight with a few girlfriends, are you? While the cats away?'

'Wow, the old boy's network is working well I see,' she said.

'It is indeed. Out to raise some hell? Lock up your sons? Does that sound about right?' he teased.

'Ha-ha, you know me,' laughed Bobbi.

'You know,' said Dave, as he grabbed a towel to wipe down the bar, 'it's funny that you objected to being called middle aged, but not a cougar.'

'Well, I'm part of the club now,' she beamed. 'These heels are only temporary until I get my leopard print ones, next week.'

'Nice. What can I get you?'

'G&T please. Oh wait, have you got ice now?'

'Yeah, of course,' he said, a little surprised.

'Huh. Tanya said your YTS told her you didn't have any.'

'Ah right,' he nodded. 'Scott told your friend that we were expecting some in. It was only going to be a few minutes, but she told him to forget it.'

'Ok, got ya,' she said, looking over at Tanya who was on her phone again. 'Tell you what then, give me a beer instead.'

'One beer for the little lady, coming right up,' he said, turning towards the fridges.

'Little lady?' she frowned. 'Have you seen my arse lately?'

'Yeah,' Dave said, turning back towards her, 'last night in my dreams.'

He shot Bobbi a winning smile.

Bobbi let out a laugh.

'Ok, the "lady" will have a beer. Thank you. Thing is,' she said, leaning closer to whisper, 'between me, you, and the wall, I don't want her seeing I've got ice. It'll just set her off and she's in a bit of mood as it is already.'

'Women's problems?' he joked.

'Yes,' said Bobbi, 'a man likely.'

As Dave stooped down and reached into the fridge to grab a green bottle, Bobbi looked over again at Tanya. Above her head, there was a framed picture of a wine holder in the shape of a baby elephant, but instead of a bottle of wine, the elephant was holding a bottle of beer. The contrast between its joyful form, and the sad demeanour of Tanya's frame was stark. Bobbi had seen this Tanya many times over the years, both in and out of work. Many hours of Bobbi's life had been spent providing an ear for Tanya to vent into.

'Here you go,' said Dave, placing the chilled bottle on the counter. 'On the house.'

'Aww, thanks Dave. Are you sure?'

'Of course. Now, are you sure you're ok to drink this with your medication?' he asked as he pointed to his temple and scrunched up his face.

'Absolutely not,' said Bobbi, 'but thank you for asking.'

'No problem,' he said, closing his eyes and giving her a slight nod.

'Hey, I'm sorry yours didn't work out though,'

she said.

Dave looked at her quizzically.

Bobbi continued, 'I mean, you diligently took them pills every day, morning and night, for six months, and here you are…still an arsehole.'

'Medicine can only do so much, I guess,' said Dave with a grin.

Bobbi spotted Alexis. She waved and pointed to where Tanya was sitting. Alexis followed Bobbi's fingers, saw Tanya, and headed over to her.

'I've got to go,' said Bobbi, 'but thanks for the drink. We'll probably call in later.'

'I'll be here,' said Dave. 'Have a good night.'

'By the way, if Scott's looking for a cougar later, tell him I said hi,' said Bobbi with a wink.

Bobbi turned and took a swig of her chilled beverage. She was relieved to see that Tanya and Alexis were chatting, Tanya looking much more engaged and alert than the imitation of a human she'd presented before.

'Hi darling,' said Bobbi to Alexis, kissing her on the cheek. 'You scrub up nice,' touching the fabric of her jacket.

'Aw thank you. It's nice to be out honestly. I'm so hungry. What time are we going to the restaurant?'

'Err,' said Bobbi, looking at her watch, 'the reservation is about half an hour, but we can head there soon if you like?'

' No, it's ok, you've just got a drink.'

'Don't worry,' said Bobbi, raising her bottle, 'this won't last long. Do you want a drink then?'

'Well,' said Alexis, glancing over at the young barman who had re-emerged, 'I might just get a softie-

'Don't,' interrupted Tanya, 'trust me, it's awful.' She handed her drink to Alexis.

'Taste that if you want.'

Alexis lifted the straw out of Tanya's glass and took a sip.

'Seems ok. A bit flat maybe, but it's pub Coke, I guess. It would be better if it had a little ice, maybe?'

'Don't...' said Bobbi, shaking her head while trying to push the words back down Tanya's throat with sympathetic eyes.

'Oh, have I missed something?' asked Alexis.

'It's fine,' said Tanya, 'that child behind the bar was just a little less than helpful earlier.'

'I used to work in a pub,' said Alexis.

'Did you?' said Tanya. 'Where was that?'

'Back at home. It was just a little village pub, not a modern place.'

'I can see you there, actually,' said Bobbi, 'all the old guys coming in, sweet talking the pretty, young thing serving them their stout.'

Alexis laughed.

'You're not far off. Most of them were sweet, but you'd always get a few grumpy gits in too.'

'A few characters, I imagine,' said Bobbi.

'Yes. There was this lovely little couple, I remember,' said Alexis, grabbing a stool and sitting as she began her story. 'Every Tuesday, the pub had a 'Pie and Peas' night, and on Sundays they'd serve Sunday lunches.'

'Ooh, I love a roastie,' said Bobbi, with a grin.

Tanya shot Bobbi a disapproving look, which landed, making Bobbi recoil slightly. She took a sip of her beer, a little narked.

'So,' Alexis continued, 'almost without fail, this couple would come in, and have the same thing every week. They were maybe in their late seventies, I guess. They would go to their table, and he'd take her coat, putting it on the nearby rack. He'd then come to the bar and order their drinks. "A white wine spritzer and a pint of ale please" he'd say. Extremely polite, hair smart, well dressed, you know what I mean. It was such a pleasure to serve him.'

'Did you only speak to him?' asked Tanya.

'Yeah, she always just sat at the table. They would chat and be laughing together. Quietly though, they weren't loud and boisterous like others can be. The only time I heard her was when they were leaving. He'd get her coat, and as they approached the door, she'd wave and say, "Thank you".'

'Aww, how sweet,' said Bobbi.

'He'd carry the drinks over to their table, and they'd clink their glasses together. It was lovely.'

'I can see Mike being like that when he's older,' said Tanya.

Bobbi was in mid-swig and just managed to stop her beer from spraying out.

'You're joking, aren't you?'

Tanya didn't reply, leaving the conversation to collapse like a kite without wind.

'Anyway,' said Alexis, 'I just always thought that was so lovely.'

'It really is. Do you know if they still go there?' asked Tanya.

'Well, it's quite sad actually,' said Alexis, 'because I spoke to my mum, sometime last year I think, and she said that his wife had died and after that, he didn't go to the pub anymore.'

'Oh no,' said Bobbi, 'that's really sad.'

Tanya nodded, wishing she hadn't asked. She took a gulp of her coke, hoping its foul taste would wipe away any sombre comparisons her mind might make.

'OMG' said Lucy quietly, as she turned into the driveway.

Lucy had finished slightly earlier than normal and went to Claire's house straight from work. She'd packed her make up and outfit for the evening, giving herself enough time to iron it if necessary and get ready so she could look her best. After a quick tour of the house, Lucy spent most of the first hour or so on her own. Claire, although technically off the clock, still had a few emails and calls to make before she was satisfied that she could call it a day.

The house was huge, with its own driveway, and four bedrooms, two with en-suites, including the one Lucy would be staying in. It was fitted throughout with modern units and furnishings, in a minimalist style. A glass coffee table, with an engraved horse's head in the centre, was gorgeous, and polished to a sparkle. It looked very expensive, at least to Lucy's mind, whose eyes were more accustomed to more modest surroundings. She was scared to place her ceramic cup on it, so decided to just hold on to it. When she arrived, a programme about some historic event was playing on the TV, but being unable to find the remote, and not wanting to disturb Claire, she'd just let it play on. It was fair to say, that Lucy was a little awe struck, and a little intimidated, by the house she was in.

As their taxi pulled away, Lucy was admiring the trimmed hedges, tidy lawns, and secure gates that accompanied many of the properties in Claire's neighbourhood.

'Penny for them?' asked Claire.

'I was just thinking about your house,' said Lucy.

'Ok. Do you like it?'

'Like it? It's bloody gorgeous. Sorry,' she said, not wanting to sound so moronic.

'Ha, thanks.'

Claire took a breath, as if to say something, when Lucy followed up.

'How did you get it? I mean is it yours or do you rent?'

'No, it's mine, it's paid for,' said Claire, her face suddenly sterner, more business-like. 'We moved in when Jonathan was born. Then when Bill moved out, I got it in the divorce.'

'Ah right. That's good.'

'Yes,' continued Claire, 'that side of things was all amicable. It made the most sense, and he could afford it. Jonathan was settled, it was good for his school, my work etc. He wasn't a dick about anything like that.'

'And does Jonathan get on ok with him?'

'He does. He was five when we split, and it's been five years, so he's gotten used to things. Plus, they do a lot of stuff together. They go to football games, watch films...a lot of things I don't really have the time to do because of work but that's fine. He's a great dad. He was just a shitty husband.'

Lucy nodded.

'It really is a beautiful house. And so clean. How do you manage that when you're so busy?'

'Well, Jonathan helps out.' Reading Lucy's confused look, Claire clarified, 'I mean he keeps his room spotless, which is how he gets his pocket money. He's a little bit like that anyway. Not from me, I have to say. That's all from his dad. But he's great at loading the dish washer, putting the rubbish out, little things like that.'

'Good lad,' smiled Lucy.

'Yes, he is. Everything else though, is Adrianna.'

'Who's that?'

'She's my little Polish helper. Just a couple of times a week, she'll come in for an hour and hoover, and polish, stuff like that. On Mondays, Tuesdays, and Thursdays, Jonathan has after school clubs, so he'll eat at school with the boarders, but on Wednesday, Adrianna comes a little later and will make dinner for us both.'

'Sounds amazing,' said Lucy.

'Oh, it is. Her food is simple, but it's delicious. Have you been to Poland?'

'No,' said Lucy, shaking her head, 'I haven't travelled far at all really.'

'Why not?' asked Claire.

'Money, I guess, but also time,' said Lucy. 'At Uni I was so busy with my studies and training. I went to Spain two years ago, in the summer for a few days to go clubbing, but I know that's not proper travelling.'

'Where do you want to go?'

'God, I don't know!'

Lucy's eyes grew wide as she thought how best to answer.

'India. America. Anywhere, really.'

'Do it!' said Claire definitively, making Lucy laugh in surprise. 'I mean it' she continued, 'the world's a big place. I mean, don't be crazy about things. You've got to be careful. Do you have friends you could travel with?'

'Yeah, there's a couple of Uni friends I've stayed in touch with.'

'Good,' Claire nodded, 'I think it's so important.'

'My mum did when she was younger,' said Lucy. 'She said it was the best time of her life.'

Lucy smiled, thinking of her mum back at home. Friday night, she'd be watching something with grandma. Lucy's dad had been working night shifts lately, so would be getting up soon. Her stomach rumbling brought her thoughts back to the prospect of dinner.

'I hope the restaurant is good. I like Tapas but haven't been to this one yet.'

Claire smiled.

'Hey, thank you for inviting me tonight.'

'Of course,' said Lucy, 'you don't have to say that.'

'No, I know but I just wanted to say thank you. You know, my work can be stressful, and it's competitive and takes up a lot of my time, so having the chance to unwind a little is great.'

Lucy smiled.

'Let's hope you're not throwing up later because of a dodgy king prawn or something.'

'Ha, Christ, let's hope not!' said Claire, beaming a smile.

The taxi pulled up outside the restaurant. As they entered, Lucy spotted Bobbi at a table in the corner and hurriedly trotted over. Claire removed her jacket and handed it to a member of staff. Bobbi stood and wrapped Lucy up in a big hug.

'Hi everyone' she beamed, tapping Alexis, who was in front of her, on the shoulder, and waving at Tanya. Seeing that Claire was now approaching behind her, Lucy said, 'This is Claire, and I'm starving.'

Everyone laughed.

'Hi, starving' said Tanya.

In the commotion of everyone getting seated, her joke was unheard. The moment having passed, it was too late to repeat it. A tiny thought crept into her mind that everyone had heard it but ignored it for being unfunny. She reached for the menu and hid behind its oversized format and bright colours.

'She's not a maid,' Claire insisted, trying to laugh it off.

Once the typical exchanges about how they'd all gotten to the restaurant, whether they'd been there before, the décor, the waiters, and what they fancied having were over, the conversation focussed on Claire briefly. She was unknown to Bobbi, Tanya, and Alexis, and so Lucy ran through how they'd met, and how beautiful Claire's house was. Claire filled them in on where she lived, playing down Lucy's revelation that Claire had a Polish maid.

'Sounds brilliant,' said Bobbi, impressed. 'I've done no housework all week while those two have been away; is she free on Sunday by any chance?'

When the waiter came to take their orders, Claire was the first to speak.

'If it's ok, ladies, I'd like to order some wine for you all, as a thank you for inviting me tonight.'

The women reacted with a mix of light protest and appreciation, but Claire insisted and engaged the waiter, enquiring about what they had. Lucy and Tanya looked over their menus a final time, while Alexis and Bobbi considered what dishes they might like to share. Claire confirmed the bottles she'd decided on with everyone, who voiced their approval. A selection of cheeses, olives, and bread were brought to the table. Lucy dived into the bread, dipping a piece into the accompanying oil.

The women each chose their starters. Lucy and

Alexis chose the Pan Tumaca (bread with olive oil, garlic, and salt), served with ham; Claire went for a black pudding dish, made with rice; Bobbi opted for croquettes filled with wild mushrooms; and Tanya picked Salmorejo, a tomatoey cold soup. The wine arrived soon after. The group hushed as a young dark eyed, and dark-haired, waiter poured them each a glass. Alexis, Claire, and Tanya each said 'gracias,' to which he replied 'de nada' demurely.

Bobbi's glass was filled next.

'Grassy arse,' she said with a cheeky smile.

The waiter's smouldering demeanour shattered as he broke out laughing. He spoke in Spanish to a passing waiter, clearly repeating the words 'grassy arse,' causing much laughter.

When he'd finished pouring, he said, in broken English, 'Thank you, enjoy your food,' before flashing a broad grin. The women all chuckled together.

'He's a bit of alright, isn't he?' said Bobbi. 'What do you think, Tanya? Would you like to give him a tip?'

'I don't know where he's been,' said Tanya drolly. Bobbi smiled, glad that the friend she'd hope to see had finally decided to show up at the party.

'Cheers ladies' she said, raising her glass.

'Cheers' they all called back, each ensuring they clinked everyone else's glass.

'Are you strict with your diet, Claire?' asked Alexis.

'No, not at all,' said Claire, 'which is another reason I like to exercise so much. I don't have time to be counting calories, and I'm not organised enough to do meal planning. I see a lot of clients, either in the office, or visiting, so I tend to eat whatever I can grab on the go. More often than not, when I get home, I order a takeaway or just pick something up that I can throw in the microwave.'

'It'd be nice to be able to waste money like that,' said Tanya.

Bobbi twitched slightly at Tanya's comment, dismayed that 'Happy Tanya' had seemingly only popped in to show her face.

Claire noticed Bobbi's reaction.

'It's not wasting money really when I'm paying for convenience. I simply don't have the luxury of time to cook every night,' she said coolly, looking directly at Tanya, who shrank a little. 'I might if I have someone round for dinner, but shopping for a long list of ingredients, and then preparing a meal is laborious. I know a lot of women enjoy cooking, baking and what have you, but I'm not one of them,' said Claire.

'I can't cook,' said Bobbi.

'Really?' said Alexis. 'I thought you made those scones you brought round to mine a couple of weeks ago.'

Bobbi shook her head.

'Nope. Bought by Bobbi, baked by Sainsbury's, the night before. I supplied the tub they were in though.'

'That's why I thought you made them,' laughed Alexis. 'Why didn't you tell me?' she asked.

'You didn't ask,' smiled Bobbi. 'By the way' she laughed, 'I didn't make the jam we had with them either.'

'Ha, yes I realised that,' said Alexis, rolling her eyes.

'When was this?' asked Tanya.

Bobbi looked at Alexis.

'Err, when was it? Last Tuesday?'

Tanya nodded but said nothing.

'Bobbi's order had arrived,' Alexis chipped in.

A hush descended as their starters arrived and they all tucked in, occasionally broken by satisfied murmurs at the deliciousness of the food.

'Do you sell cosmetics?' Claire asked Alexis.

'No, craft items. I make bespoke pieces, but I also sell supplies of stationery, and other materials.

'That's how we met,' said Bobbi, her finger pointing towards Alexis and then herself. 'My mum had been on at me to make a scrapbook of Louise's baby stuff.'

'That was ages ago,' said Tanya, 'so what was last week?'

'Just some stuff for Louise to take to the caravan,' answered Bobbi. A little tension had crept into her throat, which she cleared with a cough.

'Scrapbooking isn't a hobby for me at all, but it made my mum happy. One of those obligatory things she expects to have as a grandmother.'

'Ah yes,' said Claire. 'I'm not really that close to my parents, so it's not that much of an issue for me.'

'I'm sorry to hear that,' said Alexis.

'No, it's not something I worry about. She had very clear ideas about what I should do when I was growing up, which basically involved having children and living near to her. She was disappointed when she discovered she had a daughter that could think for herself, and that I was going to do what I wanted to do.'

'What about your dad?' asked Bobbi.

'He just wanted me to do what I wanted. He worked in finance, like I do, so maybe he'd be proud, but he left when I was away at college. He liked a drink, and other women. So understandably, there was a lot of arguing and fighting.'

'Sounds bad,' said Lucy, thinking of her own parents.

'They're just people,' said Claire. 'People fuck up, don't they, if you pardon my French.'

Bobbi nodded, liking Claire's honesty.

'They say you can't choose your family,' said Bobbi.

'Yes, and no relationship is a given,' said Claire. 'Dad lives abroad now. As for Mum, I'd never stop her from seeing Jonathan and when he's older he can choose to do what he wants, but otherwise…'

Bobbi nodded.

'I think that's fair enough,' she said. 'It's great that my mum lives so close, and she helps out loads with my daughter, but she does my head in at times, oh does she!'

'Do you have kids?' asked Claire, looking at

Alexis and Tanya.

They both shook their heads.

'Maybe one day,' said Alexis.

Tanya looked at her food and Claire didn't push for an answer.

Soon after, they had all finished their starters. Just as soon as the plates had been cleared away, the main courses began to arrive. Alexis had ordered Pescaito Frito (fried fish), while Tanya chose Paella with seafood. Bobbi ordered a Spanish omelette, while Lucy and Claire ordered a selection including Calamari, Mussels, Cuttlefish, Papas Arrugadas (boiled potatoes), and salad, with a plate of Patatas Bravas (fried potatoes) for the table to share.

'What are you like with hot food?' Claire asked Lucy, having spotted Gilda on the menu. This was a classic item consisting of a skewer with an anchovy, an olive, and a hot pepper.

'I don't mind it,' said Lucy.

Throughout her childhood, she'd tasted lots of traditional Caribbean recipes, many of which had quite a kick, especially when her grandma cooked. When her mum cooked, the food tended to be milder to suit her dad's more sensitive English palette, something that would often draw scorn from his mother-in-law.

'Cho! What is this jerk chicken?' she would bemoan, adding more spices to her own serving.

The story of the time Grandma slipped up was legendary in their house.

'So,' began Lucy, 'this one night, my mum had

made a pork curry. My dad was going out with some of his mates and would be eating later on, so mum added some heat to the dish to please grandma. The thing is, my grandma didn't *know* my dad was out, so she added extra chilli to her own plate without saying anything.'

Lucy started to laugh, tickled by the memory of what happened.

'So, I'm sat in the kitchen with my mum, and we're eating this curry, when we hear this anguished cry from the living room. "Arrgghhh, rhatid, rhatid!"' my grandma was shouting.

'What does 'rhatid' mean?' chuckled Bobbi.

'It's like, "damn" or "hell"!' said Lucy. 'So, we can hear her shouting, and *then* I hear her running. She came bursting into the kitchen. I didn't know my grandma could run, but she was! "Rhatid! Rhatid!" she was gasping, over and over. My mum's name is Femi, so grandma was panting, "Femi...what the hell...oh, rhatid!" It was so funny.'

The women were creased up.

'Was she alright?' laughed Alexis, wiping a tear from her eye.

'Yeah, she had a few long drinks. Me and mum though were just bent double.'

As they ate, conversations broke out between Lucy and Claire, and Alexis and Bobbi, who were lightly chatting about the food, plans for the rest of the evening, and this and that. Tanya, sitting on the end of the table, listened at first to Bobbi asking Alexis about her business, and clients. She was too far away from Lucy and Claire to either listen in or talk to them without talking over Bobbi and Alexis. Eventually, she just concentrated on her food, which was a little bland. The soup had been surprisingly filling though, together with the bread she'd used to mop up any remaining drops. She felt for her phone, disappointed she had not felt it vibrate in her pocket in the last hour or so. The screen confirmed there were no further messages from him. When she looked back up, her eyes caught Bobbi staring at her while she was in mid-conversation with Alexis. Tanya quickly put the phone back in her pocket, picked up her napkin and wiped the corners of her mouth.

When they'd all finished, the waiters collected their plates and Bobbi asked for the bill. Alexis took responsibility for working out who owed what, Claire again insisting that she was happy to pay for the wine.

'Shall we ask them to take a photo?' asked Lucy.

'Yes! Well done, Lucy!' said Alexis, as she started to search in her bag.

'No problem,' smiled Lucy, not sure what she had done.

Alexis retrieved a disposable camera.

'I used to use these quite often when I went on walks and things, but I remembered this one had a couple of shots left on it, so I thought I'd bring it to use it up.'

The waiter returned with their receipt, and Alexis asked him to take the snap. He stood at the far end, and Bobbi counted down. After three, he clicked and handed the camera back to Alexis. She rolled it on, only to discover it had reached its end.

'Again?' asked the waiter.

'No,' said Alexis, holding up the camera 'it's ended, err terminado.'

'Ah, terminado,' he repeated. 'Ok, thank you so much, have a good evening.'

'Where now then Bobbi?' asked Alexis, as they all stood outside.

'I think it's time for cocktails,' said Bobbi.

'Right ladies,' ordered Claire, 'this is where the night really gets going. First we start with shots.'

Lucy clapped, while Tanya groaned.

'Really?'

'Yes' said Bobbi, 'we're doing this!'

Lucy, Alexis, and Tanya found an empty booth, covered in recently used glasses. With nowhere else to sit, they started to move the glasses to a nearby ledge. A waitress quickly came over and started helping. Within a minute, the glasses were gone, and she had wiped the table clean. The waitress handed them a menu, detailing the cocktails available. The bar was well lit, with chandeliers descending from the low ceiling, and felt spacious, the space extended further than it looked from the outside. It was busy but not heaving for the time of evening, although the outside area was full, with drinkers standing gratefully beneath heaters now that the night's chill had almost completely stripped away the sun's warmth.

At the bar, Bobbi and Claire waited to be served.

'What you think, two each?' asked Claire.

Bobbi nodded.

'Go halves?' she said, passing Claire some cash.

Claire agreed.

'Five Blue Kamikazes' and 'Five Mad Dogs please,' she barked into the ear of the barman.

The shots were dutifully loaded up onto a silver tray, which Claire carried.

'Here we go ladies,' she said.

'Oh God,' said Alexis laughing, 'what's that?' pointing at the pink and white liquid.

'It's Raspberry Syrup and vodka,' said Bobbi, 'otherwise known as a "Mad Dog".'

They each picked one up and knocked it back.

'Woah,' said Tanya, 'that's strong.'

'It's lovely,' said Alexis, running her finger inside her glass and licking it.

'No resting,' said Claire, 'time for round two.'

This time they raised their shots and clinked them in unison, before sending the blue liquid tumbling down their throats.

'Ooh,' said Lucy, 'that was nice!'

The booth was within fifteen feet of a small space where a keyboard, bass guitar, and mic stand had been set up.

'That food was lovely,' said Alexis. 'I'd definitely go there again.'

Tanya nodded.

'How often do you all come out together then?' asked Claire.

'Actually,' said Bobbi, 'this is the first time.'

Claire looked surprised.

'I mean,' said Bobbi, 'me and him, just tend to have a drink at home. He's not a big drinker, so is happy just spending time with me in the house, watching a boxset or whatever.'

'And who is 'him'?' said Claire. 'Your

husband, right?'

'Yeah, his name's Mike.'

'And what about the rest of you? How about you, Tanya?' asked Claire, catching Tanya slightly off guard.

'Sorry, what did you say?' she asked, pretending she'd misheard the question.

'I said, is this your kind of scene?' asked Claire.

'It's alright,' said Tanya, with a shrug.

Claire waited for more, before sensing that that was Tanya's full reply.

'Ok,' she said.

'I think we're going to get some music,' said Lucy, seeing two men and a woman approach the instruments.

After a brief tune up, the woman introduced the group, drawing a whoop from a small crowd of supporters in the opposite corner. She acknowledged them with a wave. The keyboard player began to hit his notes, as the group launched into a rendition of "I feel the Earth move". Her voice was bright and clear, as she caressed the air around the microphone, her hands mimicking the notes in the range of her vocals. The guitarist looked young, standing stock still and head down. His only discernible movement was the flicking of his fingers against the bass strings, which he did very well. The keyboard player was middle aged, his hair cropped short to look like more as it had thinned. He wore a black shirt, and black trousers, and seemed completely in synch with the instrument he was playing. His energy translated well to those in attendance, who nodded along in time with the rhythm. The women watched on admiringly, particularly Lucy who seemed hypnotised by the singer as she shimmied and swayed, her body and voice commanding the attention of all who were in earshot. At the song's end, the crowd showed their appreciation with a chorus of cheers, applause, and whistles. Tanya took the opportunity to get up and head towards the restrooms.

'Alexis,' said Bobbi, 'get me and Tanya a drink please if you're going. I'm going to see how she is.'

Alexis nodded.

As Bobbi moved away, Alexis and the others discussed drinks before catching the attention of a passing waiter.

18

'Tanya?' said Bobbi.

The restroom had two cubicles, only one of which was vacant.

'One minute!' came the reply from behind the door. Rather than just stand around awkwardly, Bobbi checked her reflection. She had begun to reapply her lipstick, when she heard a flush, and Tanya opened the door.

'She's quite a singer, isn't she?' asked Bobbi.

'Not bad, I suppose,' said Tanya, who started to wash her hands. She looked at her face, puffing out her cheeks as if willing herself on. 'So, where've you been lately?'

'What do you mean?' replied Bobbi, unsure of Tanya's tone.

'I just feel like I haven't heard from you, you know. I've barely seen you at work, or out of it.'

'I saw you last week, didn't I?' Bobbi said defensively. 'How was the meeting by the way?'

'It was shit. They're a bunch of arseholes, like I told you, and that was three weeks ago.'

Bobbi scrambled to think where she had been. 'Was it? Well, I don't know. I've just been busy, I guess. Sometimes the days kind of blend into each other, so I don't know what I'm doing from one to the next. It's like that when you've got kids.'

'One kid, Bobbi, you've got one,' said Tanya aggressively, 'unless you're counting Mike as a kid too.'

'Hey, you haven't seen him when we haven't had sex for a few days,' joked Bobbi. 'All the toys get thrown right out of the pram.'

'I don't want to know, thanks,' said Tanya, returning to her reflection.

'Are you mad at me?' asked Bobbi.

'No, I'm not mad, Bobbi' said Tanya. 'It's just I've had all of this going on with my dad and I could have done with you being there to support me a bit. Then I hear you're going round to Alexis' for scones, or whatever, and-'

'I was picking up an order for Louise!' said Bobbi matter of factly, shedding some of her previous defensiveness.

'Ok,' said Tanya, 'but that was still just last week.'

Another woman entered the restroom, silencing them both momentarily. She moved into one of the cubicles.

'Who's been messaging you?' asked Bobbi.

Tanya's head dropped, as she moved to the hand dryers.

'No-one. It's nothing,' she said, before moving her hand beneath the blower, activating it into life.

Bobbi waited silently, not wanting to yell over the noise of the fan. Her eyes searched the small space for somewhere to rest their gaze, rather than the back of Tanya.

When the fan stopped, Bobbi asked 'Is it Lee?'

The noise of the fan filled the room again. Bobbi felt frustrated and moved closer to Tanya.

'Look, it's your business, but just try to enjoy yourself. It's a nice night, let's have a drink and a bit of fun.'

Tanya continued to look straight ahead. Despite her hands being well dried, she kept them under the machine, until it timed itself out.

'I'll see you out there,' she said finally, not looking at Bobbi, 'I'm just going to check my teeth. I can feel a bit of rice or something stuck and it's a nuisance.'

'Ok,' said Bobbi, 'see you out there.'

The entrance to the restroom was tucked away behind a side passage, so once outside, Bobbi took a moment to push down her annoyance. She pictured Alexis and Lucy's faces and allowed her mind to tap into the lyrics being sung by the vocalist, before heading back to the group.

'So, you're on your own a lot?' asked Lucy.

'Yeah,' said Alexis, 'I moved here to be nearer Paul, but I knew because of his job that he could be out of the country for a couple of months at a time. That's fine though because I'm fine being on my own. I was happy to move really.'

'Why is that?' asked Claire.

'I'm twenty-six,' she said. 'I've basically lived in the same place my whole life. So yes, he was a reason, but he wasn't the only reason. I wanted the chance to live somewhere else, see a different part of the country, and meet new people.'

Claire nodded.

'Good for you,' she said.

'Yeah,' said Lucy, 'I think my parents expect me to move out at some point, but they're not pushing me. Not yet anyway,' she laughed.

'You'll know when you're ready,' said Alexis.

'Have you met many people then?' asked Claire.

'My business is doing ok,' shrugged Alexis. 'It pays the bills and then some, so I can't complain, but the people I meet are customers rather than friends. Because of his work, Paul didn't really have a large circle of friends either that I could tap into. That's why it's been nice meeting Bobbi, and Tanya. And now, you guys,' she said with a smile.

Lucy touched Alexis' hand.

'What do you think's happening in there?' she asked.

'Not sure, but Tanya seems a bit rattled by something,' said Alexis, glancing over her shoulder. 'Oh, she's coming, I'll ask her later, ok?'

Claire and Lucy nodded.

'Hiya,' said Bobbi. 'I love this song.'

The women all smiled.

'Drinks shouldn't be too long,' said Alexis. 'I got you both a Cosmopolitan. Hope that's ok?'

Bobbi gave a thumbs up.

'Perfect darling,' she said, 'thank you.'

A few moments later, Tanya rounded the corner and headed towards them.

'Are none of your drinking?' she asked, as she settled back into the space she'd sat in before.

'On their way,' said Lucy.

'Ah, speak of the devil,' said Claire, eyeing their waiter who was carrying a tray loaded with five cool, and colourful looking, drinks.

'Two cosmopolitans,' said the waiter.

'That's ours,' said Bobbi, passing one to Tanya.

'One mojito, one margarita, and a sangria,' he announced, which went to Claire, Lucy, and Alexis, respectively.

'Right, cheers everyone,' said Tanya, to the group's surprise. 'Let's get mortal.'

Two thick, heavy looking glass doors, with wooden panel handles, provided the final barrier to the main bar of the evening. Although polished, and expensive looking, the entranceway to The Champagne Bar appeared small, the presence of a large burly man standing next to it possibly skewing its perceived proportions. A few paces ahead of the doors, a red tasselled rope joined two poles, there for symbolic value really as it looped ridiculously low to the ground to be considered any kind of deterrent. Another man flanked the rope, trimmer than the other, and arguably taller as he stood in front of the group now. Both gents, a title only assumed by the gentle manner in which one moved the rope aside, and the other opened the thick door with a slight nod in deference to every lady, wore thick black coats, with dark trousers and shoes. Their hair was uniformly short, given the impression of authority and capability, essential for the position in which they were employed. The addition of visible, yet discrete, earpieces, only added to their air of professionalism.

Bobbi, looking behind herself, saw that what had been a small queue when they joined, had doubled in size in the ten minutes or so it had taken for them to reach the front. The man at the door moved to open it as a thirty something couple exited. In doing so, the slightly distant but thudding sound of a base system precipitated the air, interspersed with the blend of chatter, laughter and merriment as can only be generated by a crowd of alcohol fuelled people in a darkened space. Lucy, standing at the front of the queue alongside Claire, had been shifting up and down constantly, partly to keep warm, but mostly out of sheer vibrancy of spirit. The sound had the effect of an adrenaline shot on her, setting her hands clapping away as she released a little squeal. Over her shoulder, she shot Bobbi a huge smile, which she, mirror-like, returned. The effect energised Bobbi, who instantly felt more focussed and connected to her body and surroundings. She stood up taller, pushing her shoulders back and her chest outwards. Wanting to check her hair, she reached for her phone.

'Come on, Lexi, quick selfie,' she said.

Bobbi slung an arm round Alexis, who stooped a little, so their faces were side by side within the camera's small screen.

'One, two, three!' Bobbi shouted as the camera clicked. A little too loudly as it happened, causing Tanya to flinch and turn around. Bobbi didn't see Tanya's disgruntled frown, as her head was down looking at the screen. The flash had failed to engage, so their faces were pitched in darkness.

'Well, that was shit,' she said. 'Come on, let's try that again. Tanya, are you getting in?'

'No!' Tanya said, without turning around.

'Suit yourself. Ok Lexi, one, two, three, cheeeese!!!!'

On three, Alexis stuck out her tongue. The blinding flash captured their likenesses this time, both teeth (Bobbi) and tongue (Alexis) clearly seen.

'Hell's teeth,' said Bobbi, 'how pale am I?'

'You're not,' said Alexis, 'it's just the lighting.'

'It's not the best angle either is it?' laughed Bobbi. 'Look at those chins.'

Alexis laughed.

'Don't be daft,' she said, 'you're gorgeous you are.'

Bobbi made a noise with her mouth, somewhere between a fart and a "you what?"

'Lexi, I think that cocktail might be starting to kick in. Play your cards right and I might take you home,' said Bobbi, laughing.

Tanya turned round again, but this time she wore a creased smile.

'What the hell are you talking about?

'I'm just letting Alexis know that I've never been with a woman, but if she was interested, which I know she isn't, she might be able to turn me.'

'I'll bear it in mind,' laughed Alexis.

Tanya rolled her eyes and turned away.

'Here,' said Bobbi, 'let's get another picture. One where I haven't got four chins please.'

The sound from within the bar filled the air again, at which point, the man by the rope leant forward and unhooked the rope.

'Too late,' said Tanya, 'we're going in.'

Holding the rope and stepping back, the man gestured to the group to go through. Claire, who had been standing at the front with Lucy, was almost as tall as the man on the gate.

'Have a good night, ladies,' he said.

'You too,' said Claire, making eye contact with him as she moved towards the now open door.

The second man didn't speak, but gave a genial nod, as they went inside.

It wasn't visible from the outside, due to the low lighting, but there was a steep staircase descending deeply and veering off to the right. The walls were decorated in a dark red, patterned wallpaper, although it was too dim to appreciate the design. The only light came from thin strips above the many framed pictures on the walls on both sides, and on the underside of each step. This was a safety feature no doubt, as well as a guide to lead the soon to be drunken revellers upwards, like rats heading for the light when ready to emerge from their nest beneath the town's streets.

20

Lucy stood on the dancefloor and closed her eyes, depriving one sense temporarily to strengthen the others. In this environment, where the light was low, the music was high, and the atmosphere was joyous, she was a spirit at ease, open to everything and relishing the exquisite power she felt inside her. It had felt like a long time since she'd experienced this. The alcohol mixing in her blood had aided her transition, but she was not out of control. Far from it. She had shifted to a place of freedom, where she gave herself permission to simply be, without inhibition.

She feasted on the energy around her, letting it flow through her, uninhabited, unimpeded, from every source, herself of it and at one with it. The pulse of bass reverberated through the floor and spiked her feet, her shoes mere conduits. The humid air kissed her skin, warming her core and sending elated cries for sweet relief to her nervous system to turn on the sprinklers, sweat coming like an ice cube melting on a summers day. Her ears took the sounds, rhythms, melodies, chatter, laughter, and words, absorbing them and producing the fuel to propel her mind back to blissful moments of true happiness; running around the garden being sprayed with a hose; crossing the finish line after seeing her mum urging her home on the final stretch; the third time she had sex, which was the first with her second boyfriend, who knew what he was doing, helping her to truly realise the overwhelming pleasure to be felt from being a woman.

With each new song, her lips mouthed the words, directing her body into shapes and expressions of fun. She opened her eyes, seeing Claire before her. Claire's arms were raised, her eyes closed too, her shoulders slinking as her hips gentled swayed. She may not have been in the same house that Lucy was in, but she was on the same street. The records were on, and she was feeling the groove. She was basking in the glow of Lucy's sun, feeling more alive than she had for years. She opened her eyes in time to catch Lucy's.

'Oh my God,' shouted Lucy, 'I love it,' as she punched the air and rocked the dancefloor.

Lucy turned to Alexis and Bobbi and waved them to come over and join her. Bobbi waved back but was happy where she was. It would take a lot more alcohol for her to go out there, but she happily bopped and slapped her hand against her thigh, while holding her vodka and coke. Tanya was at the bar. Alexis was marvelling at what she was witnessing.

She finished her drink and said to Bobbi, 'Do you mind if I go over there?'

'Crack on!' said Bobbi. 'I'll watch you from here.'

Alexis hugged Bobbi and ran over. Lucy squealed and squeezed Alexis in a tight hug.

'Let's see what you've got!' she yelled in Alexis' ear, as "Don't Stop Movin'" by S-Club 7 erupted from the speakers.

Claire took a step back, bobbing her head, and clapping her hands, as she watched these two starlets go about setting the floor ablaze.

For every Robot performed, there was a Twist, for every Vogue, a Moonwalk. They cupped their ears to the DJ and touched the sky. They danced until they were breathless, their faces a picture of pure joy.

Tanya watched them from the bar, knocking back the third of five shots she'd bought.

21

Claire and Bobbi stood close together, huddled by the side of the building. They were out of the breeze that had whipped up since they'd been indoors but were still susceptible to the chilly air.

'The funny thing is,' Bobbi said, 'is that I hate that I smoke. It repulses me. In fact, my only saving grace is that I only smoke occasionally. Like when I'm out like this. I blame you.'

'Can I remind you that these are your cigarettes?' said Claire. 'Not only that, but you asked me if I wanted to come out for one?'

Bobbi considered Claire's argument but could not conjure a compelling response.

'Yeah, what's your point?' she said.

'Checkmate! Put that in your pipe and smoke it!' said Claire, smiling as she gave Bobbi the finger. She took a deep puff and blew a plume of smoke up into the air.

'Fuck!' said Bobbi, shaking her head. 'Did you say you were a lawyer or something?'

'Mortgage advisor,' Claire stated.

'You should consider the bar,' said Bobbi, 'you'd be top notch.'

'Have you ever given up before?' asked Claire, taking another draw before passing it back to Bobbi.

'Oh maybe, three, four times a day.'

'I was talking about smoking,' laughed Claire.

Bobbi's brain caught up and she let out a howl, slapping Claire on the arm.

'Sorry, yes I have, when I had Louise. It was really easy but then I wasn't smoking like a pack a day.'

'Do you ever smoke at home?' asked Claire.

'No. Smoking, absolutely not. Drinking? Yes, absolutely! How about you?'

Claire shrugged.

'The same really. I tried it when I was a kid and didn't like it. I enjoyed being active and playing sports too much, so smoking was fucking pointless.'

'So, why do you smoke now?' asked Bobbi.

'Why not?' shrugged Claire. 'Actually,' she said, 'there's just something nice about having a cigarette when you've had a drink. If there was ever a time, I was going to really start smoking it would have been when I was married.'

'Eesh!' said Bobbi, pulling a face. 'That bad huh?'

Claire scrunched up her nose.

'Yeah, but the thing is, at the time it feels like the worst thing that can happen.' She drew and blew out another gust. 'But when you've had a bit of time and put some distance between all the shit you felt and what you went through, you wonder how you didn't realise the mistakes you were making. At some point you manage to take all that anguish, and all those fears you have about yourself, doubts you could call them, and they all just, connect into something you can accept, and be at peace with.'

Bobbi nodded.

'At the end of the day, we were too similar,'

continued Claire. 'There was plenty of lust, and he was successful and all that. Money wasn't an issue, and it can be nice, you know. But we were both takers and not willing to give enough. So, it fell apart, and then it didn't take long for us both to admit that the thing was unfixable.'

'I'm not saying this to rub it in or anything,' said Bobbi, 'so please don't take this the wrong way, but I know I'm really lucky to have Mike. I don't know what impression you've got from me tonight, but this here,' she said, pointing at herself, 'can be hard work at times. And Mike, bless him, has so much joy in him. I rely on it all the time. It could have been really different mind,' said Bobbi, stubbing out the fag against the wall.

'Whys that?' asked Claire.

'Well, Mike had a pretty difficult childhood. His dad worked away, I mean away-away, like abroad. When Mike was young. I don't mean like a baby; he was, eleven or twelve, I think. Anyway, there was an accident on site and his dad died from his injuries. I mean, can you imagine?'

Claire shook her head, looking at Bobbi gravely.

'Anyway, he had a counsellor, through school and all that. He told me that his counsellor, this kindly, older man, encouraged him to make a habit of noting down anything positive. He told Mike to write down three things from every day. It didn't matter what it was, maybe something he did well, or was grateful for, or happy about. Anything really. Then at the end of the week, they would have a session, looking over his notes and celebrating his achievements. Eventually, like I say, it became a habit, which Mike carried on. I struggled when Louise came along you know.'

'That's normal,' said Claire. 'I'm honest enough to say, that kids weren't in my plans. I was too self-centred for that. It's amazing I got married,' she laughed, 'but like I said, you realise your mistakes in hindsight.'

'But now?' asked Bobbi.

'Oh,' said Claire, 'he's my absolute fucking world. I love him to bits. I know I'm not the most present or greatest hands-on mum, but I couldn't be prouder, and I make sure, at least, that he knows that. I tell him all the time.'

'Well, it was hard when Louise was born,' said Bobbi, 'but you know, Mike got us through it. We got this routine going where every Saturday night, we'd celebrate having survived a week as parents, with our child, happily, still alive. And I mean we celebrated everything. Every hour of sleep, first three hours, then four, then five. Every shitty nappy dealt with, and every meal kept down. Not just the hard things, Mike made sure we recognised every smile or laugh, her first steps, words, all that stuff. You know, I tease him all the time for being a bit of a dork and being so cheesy.'

'Ha-ha, is he?' laughed Claire.

'Oh God, yes,' said Bobbi, 'he's bloody cheese on toast! But all my winging is half-hearted in truth. I sent him a Valentine's Day card one year, and I said he was "the silver lining for my pessimistic clouds".'

'Very nice!' said Claire. 'Speaking of which, let's get back inside. I don't like the look of those clouds over there.'

22

The man on the gate had seen Bobbi and Claire go for a cigarette, so when they returned, he let them back through without question. Likewise, after raising their stamped hands for inspection, the man on the door granted them entry. The staircase had been a little tricky to tackle on the way up, alcohol causing Bobbi's sense of balance to malfunction, but exposure to the night air had revitalised her a little, ensuring the return downward journey was completed without incident.

Alexis was sat with Tanya. Bobbi had spent most of the last hour, before popping out with Claire, revelling in the sight of Lucy and Alexis throwing shapes, and so hadn't paid much attention to Tanya. She was slightly shocked to see a collection of empty shot glasses and a drained glass near Tanya's side of the table.

'You ok?' she asked them both, but more aimed at Tanya.

'We're having a great time, thank you,' said Tanya.

Claire had spotted an opening at the bar, and now returned with a tray containing five glasses of dark liquid. She placed them on the table. Tanya reached for one, but Claire moved to stop her.

'Take one' she said, 'but don't drink it yet. Lucy mentioned earlier that she had a game or something she wanted to play.'

'Ok Mum,' said Tanya, laughing alone.

Claire gave her a slight glare, before looking out at the dancefloor. 'Is she still out there?'

'Yes,' said Bobbi, 'she's talking to some lad.'

Bobbi showed Claire where Lucy was. She looked happy enough, although the man she was talking to was stumbling slightly. He gestured towards his ear, leaning down a little. As she moved closer to speak, he swivelled and tried to plant a kiss on her lips. She pushed away, but he reached for her again. Claire saw this and shot off towards her. One of the man's friends, stronger and less drunk, had intervened by the time Claire got there, but it didn't stop her shoving him, causing him to trip over his own feet and fall clumsily onto his arse. From the floor, he hurled abuse at Claire who stood unmoving, burning a hole through him with her stare. His friend picked him up and gave him a dressing down. A couple of other guys tried to move him on, but he pushed them away, and sulked off, embarrassed at what had just happened.

'I'm sorry about that,' said the man, to both Lucy and Claire.

'You need to have a word with your fucking friend there,' said Claire angrily.

'I know, and I will,' he said. He looked at Lucy, 'Are you ok?' he asked.

'Yes, I'm fine,' she said with a smile, relatively bemused by the whole spectacle.

'Ok,' he said. 'Again, I'm sorry.'

He gave a respectful nod to Claire, before heading back to his group.

Claire and Lucy went back over to the table. Bobbi and Alexis began consoling Lucy, but she played the whole thing down, laughing at the tit the guy had made of himself when he fell over.

'Thank you, Claire,' she said, who smiled back, already beginning to calm down.

Now all sitting together, Claire reminded Lucy about the game she mentioned. She had an app, where everyone would be asked a random question, which they had to either answer, or take a drink. If they drank though, they were out of the game.

'I'll go first,' said Lucy.

She pressed the question button, causing a pack of cards to be shuffled on screen. One was then selected.

'Who is your best friend?' she read. 'That's easy,' she smiled, 'mum.'

'Aww,' said Bobbi, 'me too.'

'Really?' said Tanya.

'Yes,' said Bobbi, looking perplexed.

'Ok,' said Tanya, with a shrug.

Bobbi looked at the others, who seemed a little uncomfortable.

'I'll go next,' said Bobbi, forcing her voice to be light, 'if they're all as easy as that.' The cards shuffled again, and Bobbi's question appeared.

'How old were you when you lost your virginity?' read Lucy.

The others laughed.

'Oh, I see,' said Bobbi, 'I didn't know they were going to be these kinds of questions. Let me see what this app is called.'

Bobbi looked for a moment and then burst out laughing.

'It's called "Spit or Swallow",' which made them all laugh.

'Stop stalling,' urged Claire, 'how old were you?'

'I was nineteen. I made Mike wait six months,' said Bobbi.

'That's bullshit!' said Tanya, suddenly showing interest. 'What about that lad in Spain you told me about? You were seventeen then.'

'Well,' said Bobbi, 'that's right, but that was abroad, so it doesn't count.'

The game continued in a jovial spirit, with each taking a turn, except Tanya who sullenly sat in the corner.

Alexis was asked "Who was the most foul mouthed in the group?" She answered "Bobbi", who with a huge smile told her to "fuck off". Claire was asked what her magic number was. When she said "eight", they all agreed that was respectable. Alexis was asked a question about sex toys, which she refused to answer, choosing to swallow her drink in one go. Lucy also made her drink disappear, after refusing to nominate who she would "Kiss, Marry, and Kill" in the group.

'Let me answer one,' said Tanya.

Bobbi looked a little surprised, but nodded, so Lucy passed her the phone.

'Ok, it says this is a group question, where all

other players have to answer for me. You're good at that, Bobbi.'

Bobbi's face went hard.

'It says, "What is my greatest weakness?"'

She looked at them all, but no one wanted to answer.

'Press it again,' said Bobbi, 'there's better questions than that.'

'No,' said Tanya, 'I think it's a valid question. It's just a bit of fun, right? Lucy, what do you think?'

Lucy looked at Claire, and then the others. 'Well, we've just met tonight, so I don't really know you that well. I'd maybe say, you can't handle alcohol too well.'

Bobbi let out a snort.

'Good, yes that's right,' said Tanya. 'What about you, Alexis?'

Alexis held her glass up.

'I'm empty,' she said, 'I'm out of this game.'

'Cop out!' spluttered Tanya. She turned to Claire.

'How about you?'

Claire stared at her, before picking up her glass, and sinking her drink.

'I'm out too,' she said.

Tanya stared ahead at Bobbi.

'And you? Are you out too, Bobbi?'

Bobbi nodded.

'Fine,' said Tanya. 'I think I want to go home now.'

She climbed out from her seat and without

waiting for the others, marched quickly towards the exit.

Bobbi looked at the group, feeling embarrassed. 'We'd better get out of here,' she said quietly. 'Lexi, are you ok getting a taxi with her still?'

'Yes, of course,' said Alexis, nodding.

They gathered their things, Claire polishing off Tanya's drink before they headed out together.

Outside, Tanya had crossed the road and was heading towards the taxi ranks. They quickly caught up with her.

'Tanya!' shouted Bobbi. 'You're getting a taxi with Alexis remember, or have you forgotten?'

Tanya stopped and looked at them all.

'I think you owe Lucy an apology,' said Claire firmly.

'Err, who the fuck are you, thinking you can tell me what to do?' said Tanya, angrily.

'Ok, now that's enough!' said Bobbi, raising her voice on the last word as Tanya turned her back and moved towards the taxi ranks.

'Claire' said Bobbi, turning and taking a step towards her and the rest of the group, 'I'm sorry, she's being completely out of order.'

The word 'sorry' caught Tanya's ear, stopping her sharply. She pivoted and moved closer to them all until she was only a few feet away.

Claire gave a hard smile.

'Hey, don't worry about it. I deal with women like that all day long.'

'Hey, hey, hey, hey, don't you apologise for me,' stammered Tanya, as she jabbed a finger at the air in front of Bobbi.

'I'm apologising,' said Bobbi, 'because you're embarrassing-'

'What?' interrupted Tanya. 'Am I embarrassing you? I'm embarrassing *you*!'

The group stood silent for a moment, temporarily paralysed by the ever-escalating awkwardness.

'Am I an embarrassment to you, Bobbi, huh?'

'No, you're embarrassing yourself.'

Bobbi took a breath.

'I'm sorry, but the way you've carried on tonight has been…'

Tanya released a sad, angry laugh.

'What, Bobbi? You tell me what I've been,'

raising her voice and throwing her arms into the air like a drunken composer.

'Pathetic!' said Bobbi, her voice low and direct. 'And do you want to know why?'

'Tell me,' Tanya said quietly.

'Because everything has to be a drama with you. You can't just focus on the now, and enjoy yourself, or think that maybe, you know, other people might want to just enjoy themselves, and maybe not have to suffer because you want to.'

Tanya shook her head.

'I can't believe what you're saying to me, you know what I've been through.'

Bobbi exploded, 'You've been through nothing, Tanya! Nothing!'

Tanya staggered, startled, and unbelieving not only what she was hearing but also who it was coming from.

Bobbi continued, 'You know, you mope about, about this or that. But these 'problems,' well, most of the time, they're problems of your own making. They're insignificant, and I'll tell you something else, I'm fucking tired of it. I'm tired of you whining on all the time, bringing people down with all your bullshit. It's exhausting.'

Tanya's face flushed and her eyes stung with tears, as she tried to reply.

'My Dad is-'

'Happy, Tanya!' said Bobbi. 'He's happy where he is. Accept it, for fuck's sake.'

'And I MISS HIM, ok!' Tanya shouted. 'Why is

that such a fucking problem, Bobbi?'

Quieter now, she said 'I'm a good person and I struggle sometimes. Clearly, that doesn't mean anything to you,' her voice breaking further with a layer of bitterness.

'No, no, no,' Bobbi jumped back in, 'don't give me that. We've known each other for a long time. A long time! And I have always been there for you. Supporting you, listening, encouraging you, so don't give me that bullshit ok. Just don't!'

'Hey,' said Alexis, moving slowly toward the two women like a soldier approaching an IED. 'Why don't we just all take a minute and calm down, ok?' she pleaded, desperately trying to bring an end to what was happening in front of her.

Tanya ignored her.

'I'm a good person, Bobbi!' she shouted, emotion causing her voice to break further.

'You're bloody intolerant, Tanya!' Bobbi retorted. 'That's your problem.'

Claire stepped forward, holding her hand up like a trainer throwing in a towel to signal the end of a fight.

'Come on,' she said to Bobbi in a low voice, 'walk away now.'

'How the hell am I intolerant?' roared Tanya. 'What do you mean?'

Alexis moved in front of Tanya now, trying to make eye contact with her.

'What does she mean, Alexis? How am I intolerant?'

'You're not,' said Alexis, trying to placate her. 'Let's just leave it for a bit, ok?'

Tanya shook her head.

'No,' she said belligerently, 'I want to know what she means. Bobbi!' she shouted as she moved past Alexis. 'What do you mean I'm intolerant?'

Bobbi had sat down on a nearby bench and was looking down, shaking her head slightly with the feeling of a headache coming on. Tanya moved closer to her now, close enough to block the light from the lamppost above them.

'Tanya, go away.'

'Tell me what you meant,' said Tanya curtly.

Bobbi continued to look down. She gave a large sigh, the words queuing up in her throat like sombre soldiers who knew that no good would come from their deployment.

'You expect too much of people.'

'Do I?' Tanya replied, sarcastically.

'Yes, you do. You like to think of yourself as this virtuous, and patient, and tolerant person, but you're not, and it's sad. It's like you set yourself up to fail. You always think the worst of people, and all it does is it just pollutes the way that you perceive them. And so, rather than being tolerant, you're intolerant. All the time.'

Bobbi stood up now, lifted by adrenaline as the words continued to come.

'It's like you can't just accept that sometimes, people might have had a shitty day, and so if they don't smile when you enter the room, it has to mean they're judging you. You know, people can say stupid, insensitive shit, and later apologise, if, if you gave them the chance. That's ok, you know.'

'I see,' said Tanya, nodding stiffly.

'Except you don't, Tanya. You just add it to this negative little world you've created for yourself, where you're constantly embattled, and disappointed by your lot in life and everyone around you that's in it. I mean, fuck, if someone did apologise, you probably wouldn't even accept it. So, what is the point? I just don't get it.'

Tanya took a step back in silence, absorbing Bobbi's words. They pierced her like acid melting through snow.

'It's sad Tanya, it really is,' said Bobbi sombrely, 'but it's draining. So, draining. You make yourself fucking miserable and it makes everyone around you fucking miserable.'

'Bobbi,' said Alexis, 'that's not helpful,' her words tinged more with unease and pity than an attempt to scold.

Bobbi looked at Alexis. She felt exhausted having unburdened herself of the frustrations she'd released, her energy swept away. Now, in the vacuum left behind where she stood, she looked as though her knees may buckle. She looked at Lucy, who was standing like a rabbit in the headlights, frozen into silence. Claire caught her eye and gestured that Bobbi walk with her. She acquiesced and began to move.

'Mike deserves better,' whispered Tanya.

Bobbi stopped in her tracks with Claire stood close to her side.

'What was that?' she growled, a new wave of anger rising within her.

Bold as brass, Tanya stood up straight.

'I said, Mike deserves better.'

Bobbi turned around now and glared at Tanya, who didn't flinch.

'So' Tanya continued, 'you can take your bloody opinions of me, and all my flaws, and my sodding intolerance, and you can go to hell, Bobbi! Poor Mike can put up with you because I'm out, right? That poor sod deserves better, and so does Louise!'

Petulantly, she tossed her middle finger up and held it out in front.

'Fuck you bitch!' she spat.

A sardonic smirk snaked across Bobbi's mouth, as the wave hit land.

'Oh, I see,' said Bobbi, her tone dripping in venom, 'we're going to go there are we?'

She straightened as disdain poured into her spine, setting faster than concrete and awakening a type of confidence that Bobbi rarely aired, for good reason.

'Well,' she said, gesturing to the others, 'this will be interesting.'

Claire remained close to Bobbi but was silent, Alexis likewise.

'Well come on then, Tanya,' said Bobbi, her eyes fixed now on her target, 'why don't you tell us all why Mike, and my fucking child,' she shouted, emphasising her cursing, 'deserve better?'

Tanya met Bobbi's stare, having decided the gloves were truly off.

'Well for starters, I'm not sure how he managed it to be honest,' Tanya said coldly, 'I mean, would you fuck you, Bobbi?'

She pretended to grab her own stomach and shook it while blowing her cheeks out.

Bobbi laughed.

'Really? Your skinny arse, who is terrified of dicks, is going to try to tell me how to please my, fucking, man?'

She gave a smile-less laugh.

'Mike' she stated sternly, circling her hand over and around her body, 'fucking loves this. He loves nothing more than grabbing this, and this' said Bobbi, squeezing her gut and backside.

Tanya stepped back in revulsion.

'God, you're vulgar' she said.

Bobbi stepped forward.

'Who's been texting you, Tanya?' she asked. 'Or not texting you, should I say.'

'Shut up!' said Tanya.

'I bet it's Lee. I'm right, aren't I?' Bobbi probed.

Tanya's head dropped instinctively, feeling shame at the mention of his name, exposing an open secret, which she'd tried to convince herself no one knew.

Bobbi smiled, knowing from Tanya's reaction that she'd landed a blow.

'You know,' said Bobbi, standing close to Tanya now and speaking quietly, 'even though that poor bastard couldn't get far enough away, I don't know what's sadder really; the fact that he only responds to your messages, because he wants, despite everything, for you to move on and be ok, or the fact that you just can't.'

For a moment, Tanya was speechless. Seeing Tanya on the ropes, Bobbi pushed further.

'Maybe Lee isn't the problem? Maybe, it's actually you? I'd tell you to talk to your dad about it, but he's not here either is he?'

Tanya's head jerked up, her eyes wide and filled with renewed fury. Bobbi turned and began to move away when Tanya found her voice.

'I wonder what Mike would think about that night!' she shouted.

'What night?' asked Bobbi, irritated.

'The office party,' said Tanya, pausing before adding, 'and Steve.'

Bobbi swallowed down the bile rising in her throat.

'Not that it's any of your fucking business, but actually, I told Mike.'

'Yeah? What did you tell him?' asked Tanya, eager to strike but holding off from pulling her trigger.

'That I fucked up!' said Bobbi.

She turned to the others.

'I got hammered, and ended up necking on, stupidly, with this fucking dimwit. But you know what,' she said, turning back to Tanya, 'fuck you Tanya, because I felt so guilty about that, and I told Mike, and he forgave me.'

Immediately, Tanya fired back. 'You're such a fucking liar, Bobbi. You didn't just neck on with the guy. You fucked him!'

Claire stepped forward now, between Tanya and Bobbi.

'Right, I've heard enough,' she said, giving Alexis the eyes to move towards Tanya.

'You're a disgrace, Tanya' said Claire, her voice teeming with contempt. 'Go home, have a fucking hard word with yourself, and then you can apologise tomorrow.'

'Apologise for what?' shouted Tanya, throwing her arms up. 'She should be apologising to Mike. He's the poor sod who has to always wonder whether his daughter is really his.'

'Tanya!' shouted Alexis.

Epilogue

'Did you have fun?' asked Bobbi.

' Yeah,' said Louise. 'Twix is a bit grumpy, but Alexis says it's because he's old.'

'Well, that's what happens when you get old?' said Bobbi.

'Is that why grandma is so grumpy?'

Bobbi laughed.

'Grandma gets grumpy for lots of reasons.'

Louise had spent most of the day out with Alexis working on a school project about the local area.

'Did you get your work finished?' asked Bobbi.

'Nearly,' said Louise, lifting a ring binder out of a plastic bag. 'We went to the library, and I got to talk to Pam. She let me stamp some of the books, but I got ink on my fingers. Look.'

Louise held her hand up for her mum to see.

'Oh no, do you know what that means?'

'No?' said Louise.

'It means I have to take you back in three weeks because you belong to the library now.'

'Nooo!' said Louise, 'I don't want to live there.'

'Tell you what,' said Bobbi, 'if you go and wash your hands, we'll make it our little secret. I won't tell if you won't. Ok?'

'Ok,' said Louise with a big smile, two of her teeth clearly missing.

'Go on then,' said Bobbi.

Bobbi picked up the binder and opened it.

There were photocopies inside of stories from the local newspaper, some of which had been circled with a yellow highlighter. Bobbi also saw a plastic folder, which contained two photo lab envelopes. She flicked through the first one, which had pictures of a local church, fields, cows and so on. The second envelope contained more of the same but as Bobbi flicked through, she was shocked to find one that stood out.

Louise returned holding her hands out, her hands still wet.

'All done,' she said.

Bobbi looked up. She put down the photo and inspected her daughter's hands.

'Great, you just need to dry them know darling.' Louise wiped her hands on her clothes.

'Not like…oh, never mind.'

'Who's that?' asked Louise, picking up the photo.

'Well,' said Bobbi, 'that's Alexis.'

Louise looked closer.

'Oh yeah,' she said. 'Is that you, mummy?'

'Yes, it is.'

'Your hair looks funny,' said Louise.

'Yeah, well it was three years ago darling. It's grown a bit since then.'

Bobbi pointed

'That's Lucy, you might not remember her, but you've met her before. She went to America and works there now. That's Claire, she was Lucy's friend.'

Bobbi hesitated.

'And who's that lady?' asked Louise.

'That's Tanya. You might remember her too because she was mummy's friend, but she's not anymore.'

'Why aren't you friends anymore?' asked Louise.

'Just because,' said Bobbi. 'Sometimes, people grow apart, and they stop being friends, but they make new friends and are happier.'

Louise stroked Bobbi's hand.

Bobbi kissed the top of her head.

'Go and ask Dad what we're having for dinner.'

'Ok,' said Louise. 'Dadddd,' she shouted, 'what are we having for dinner!,' her voice trailing off as she ran.

Bobbi looked at the photo again for a moment. She popped it in her pocket before putting the others back in the envelope, inside the binder.

Alex Mayberry lives and works in the historic city of Durham, in the UK. This is his second short story, after 'Yes. No. Sorry. I love you.' in November 2020, and his first poetry book, 'Letters to Madame', in August 2021.

You can follow Alex on Facebook and Instagram: @alexmayberrythefirst

For more info, please visit: alexmayberry.wixsite.com/alexmayberrythefirst

Book cover design by Juliana Ristova.
For more of her work, please visit: julianaristova.com

Printed in Poland
by Amazon Fulfillment
Poland Sp. z o.o., Wrocław

86032037R00083